Forever With You

Misfit Tattoo: Book One

By Jennifer Labelle

Forever With You

Limitless Publishing, LLC
Kailua, HI 96734
www.limitlesspublishing.com

Formatting: Limitless Publishing

ISBN-13: 978-1-64034-598-0
ISBN-10: 1-64034-598-1

Dedication

For Weldy,

It's amazing how a few simple words can change everything, isn't it?

Many years ago, our family lost two people tragically, only months apart. We lost my mother first, then you lost your son. I guess I just wanted to let you know your kind words at Nanny's funeral meant a lot. Losing my grandmother felt like losing a piece of my mother all over again, but this time, it was your story that helped me through it. It was nice to hear that I helped you cope with the loss of your son with only a few words, even all those years later.

An act of kindness can do wonders, and I thank you for sharing that with me.

"It takes a great deal of courage to see the world in all its tainted glory and still to love it."
~Oscar Wilde~

Chapter One

~A misfit refers to a person who doesn't quite fit into the social classes of today. They're a strong-minded bunch of introverts who have few friends and tend to be misunderstood.~

TOBY

Change sucked balls. He knew that first hand, and he had no choice in the matter. His life was a mess of old scars, distractions, and work. His old shop, Blank Canvas, was now Misfit Tattoo, thanks to that fucking fire that destroyed his life and his love. The one night that was supposed to be one of the happiest in his life was now nothing but a nightmare he'd never, ever forget. God only knew he'd tried time and time again. If only he could go back, get a do-over.

Toby James stood outside in the empty car lot beside the new and improved version of the shop he owned and ran his fingers through his hair as the memories came crashing back to him once more.

EIGHTEEN MONTHS EARLIER…

As soon as she entered the shop, Toby began to serenade her with Christmas songs. He was in such a good mood and couldn't wait to get their night started.

"Okay, okay, just please stop." Carley giggled. "And please, for the love of God, don't quit your day job."

His beautiful girlfriend had shown up at Blank Canvas afterhours as he'd instructed her to do to finally get the piercings she kept talking about but never had the guts to go through with.

Tonight, she'd be leaving with two brand new nipple piercings to go along with her nose ring and eyebrow ring.

Most importantly, she was also there to receive the surprise he refused to give her any hint about, and if all went according to plan, it'd be fucking epic.

She approached the back door and knocked, only to be pulled in right away and twirled around in his embrace, as he sang to her. It was the type of pussy romance shit he teased the guys about all the time, but he couldn't care less. She was his world.

"Come on, Carley, where's your spirit?" Toby asked.

"You're adorable." She smiled.

"Uh-huh. Before the night is through, we'll have five golden rings on you. Are you ready?"

"As much as I'll ever be, and I'm pretty sure you

meant to say four."

"I know what I said." Toby stood back, slipped his hands from around her waist, and held her hand as he led the way to the front of the store. The curtains were drawn, the closed sign was flipped on the door, and it smelled a little like antiseptic. His home sweet home, away from home.

He led her to her very own chair and stepped between her legs as she sat. Cupping the sides of her face tenderly, he bent over to capture her mouth against his. His soft, plump lips coaxed Carley's own to open. His teeth nipped at her bottom lip and sucked on it before his tongue sought entry, and it made her moan and squirm for him.

Her hands slid up his chest to the nape of his neck, her fingers slid through his soft, silky hair, and she tilted her head to the side even more to enjoy the wet, silky warmth of his tongue as it moved against her own. His cock swelled and pressed up against her chest, rock hard and aching, and his hips instinctively moved, allowing her to feel how she affected him. Toby moaned; he couldn't get enough of her. This chick did things to him that no other could or ever would. They clicked. Two kindred spirits joined, but there was a job to do. He pulled back from the kiss, pressed his forehead against hers, and groaned. "As much as I want to continue—" He rubbed his lower half against her again. "We should get these piercings done before it gets too late. I've got plans for the two of us. Rain check on the make-out session?"

"That depends. Do these plans include continuing what you just started?" She pouted.

"I'm aching over here." Her hands left him to trail along her chest. She cupped each breast and trailed one of her hands lower again. Teasing him, she spread her legs while he stood there captivated and drooling and rubbed herself in between them.

"Fuck! Take off your shirt." Toby growled, "Bra too, babe." He turned away from her momentarily to set up and calm himself down. There was a time and place for everything, and as much as he'd like to slide into that warm tight pussy right then and there, he had a couple of piercings to do and some things to get off his chest first. Then he'd be glad to give her anything she desired. He loved tasting her, exploring her body, and fucking her. Hell, if all went according to plan, he'd be able to do so for a lifetime.

"Yes, sir!" He smirked when she saluted him.

They'd met three years earlier in the very same spot she was in right then. Only she'd come in to get her very first tattoo at the time. She'd been too chicken shit to get anything large and opted for a small, blue butterfly on her left shoulder. There was an instant attraction, and she was so easy to be around that when he asked her out, her answer was an instant yes, and the rest was history.

"Now what?" Carley bit her lip, and he could instantly tell she was nervous about the procedure.

"Now it's showtime." Toby slowly applied an alcohol swab against each nipple and smiled when they hardened for him. Next, he grabbed a marker to mark the spot where the hole was going to go so the entry and exit holes aligned properly at the base of the nipple.

"Um, what the heck is that?" She stiffened as he reached over to grab the tool he was about to pierce her with. It sort of resembled a clamp.

"Relax, baby. It's just a device we use to hold the tissue firmly together. We've got to line up the two dots I just marked on you as closely together as possible. It should only be another minute, and we'll move on to the next one." He winked. "You good?"

She nodded and continued to bite her lip while eyeing the needle closely.

Before she knew it, the clamp was being removed, the needle went through, the loop was in, and her eyes shot wide. She hissed when it went through. There was a slight discomfort, but she took it like a champ. What took mere seconds felt like minutes, and he started on the second one.

"It stung for a minute, but these are actually quite nice." She took a few minutes to compose herself when both breasts were done and then stood in front of the floor-length mirror to have a look at her new body bling.

Toby watched her admire his work, stepped up behind her, and wrapped his arms around her midsection. "They're looking hot, babe. Then again, your tits were always pretty spectacular."

She leaned back and giggled as he dipped his head down to press his lips at the side of her neck before slowly moving them back up against her earlobe to whisper, "They'll be sore for a few days, but after that, I can't wait to show you how good they'll feel. I love that you came to me for this." He sucked her lobe inside of his mouth and looked up again to admire her. "Make sure your hands are clean when you handle the piercings and apply a good amount of soap on your nipples and on the jewelry, washing them off with warm water a few times a day to keep the area clean."

"Will do." She smiled and finally turned into his arms to face him directly. "Now, I believe you were saying you had plans for the two of us tonight. Please tell me we don't have to go far because, sore or not, I still want to continue what we started earlier, and I want to keep my shirt off for a while."

"Now that I can oblige." He laughed. "Follow me." Toby led her into his office.

It was show time.

He walked ahead to his desk, took a deep breath, and pulled the ring out of the top drawer. This was it, the official start to their forever. He walked back around the desk to a speechless Carley and lowered himself on bended knee before her. The room was dimly lit by candles he had sparked just before she arrived, and it was about as romantic as it was going to get, simple but sweet. He gulped nervously, and she surprised him by singing out, "Five golden ri—inngs," with a smile. It made the moment that much more perfect, that much more memorable.

He got up to stand in front of her instead because fuck tradition and lightly touched each ring, starting with her eyebrow, her nose, and then lightly caressing each nipple piercing. He then held up the last one reserved for her finger. "Carley, I love you, baby. Will you please marry me?"

"Yes," she cried as she jumped into his arms with delight. "I love you so much."

"Me, too. Merry Christmas, honey," Toby whispered, and he slipped the ring on her finger.

Lifting her into his arms, he carried her over to his very comfortable sofa and fulfilled his earlier promise to show her how much she was loved by making love.

The images burned into his mind like an instant replay. Every pleasure-filled moment now etched into one painful memory, because what was supposed to be the beginning of a happy life with the one person who made him feel whole turned out to be the end of it all.

His perfect fucking night became an introduction to his own personal hell. It made him wonder why he had to light those stupid candles instead of keeping the lights on? And why was he batshit enough to fall asleep before making sure they were all blown out first? But, most of all, why had he survived, and she hadn't?

A little while later, sweat poured down his brow, his breathing was laboured, and he woke up disoriented, naked, and weak.

Tired, so fucking tired.

Toby's eyes opened and closed a few times before he got his second wind. The sweet smell of Carley was gone and was replaced by the stench of something burning. Hot, why was it so hot in here? Orange lights flickered back and forth between a thick, black shield of—Holy shit! Was that smoke?

"Carley?" he croaked and coughed. "Carley, honey, wake up."

There was no response, so he nudged her. "Baby, we've got to get out of here." He shifted upright to try and get her moving, but all it did was force her to roll onto the floor. His beautiful angel wasn't moving, and he could feel himself being pulled under the moment he finished retching up a lung, but he refused to give up. All that mattered was getting the two of them out of there, like, five minutes ago. What felt like an eternity was probably mere seconds, a minute tops, when he rolled himself off the couch and onto the ground. He managed to stay low as he dragged the two of them out of his scorching office and into a slightly cooler area of the shop before it all went black again.

Toby squeezed his eyes shut and shivered as he thought about it, because the next time he woke up that night, cool air hit his face. He was able to breathe a little better thanks to the oxygen mask strapped to his face. But Carley was gone. Just like that, taken away in death.

Sirens flared in the background as they rushed him to the emergency room, and to this day, his stomach dropped every time he heard the noise of an ambulance drive by. Her loss was worse than the burns he'd endured trying to save them, and the scars, both physical and emotional, were a constant reminder that love was for suckers, and the hurt just wasn't worth the risk a second time around.

Love, commitment, and happily ever afters? Fuck that shit!

He was no fool. Only the good die young, and, well, he'd made damn sure Heaven was going to wait a long time for him ever since. Between the booze, the line-up of women to keep his bed warm, and getting his new shop up and running, he kept busy and, better yet, distracted.

Chapter Two

TOBY

"Hey, man. Are you okay?" Carson, one of his best artists, and an even greater friend, asked as he approached, bringing Toby back to the present.

"Yeah," he said. "Just need to unwind, I think." He ran his fingers through his hair again and took a deep breath. "It's good to see business is booming already, huh?" He needed a subject change to steer clear of this emotional shit going on inside of him, and there was no better subject than Misfit to break the ice.

The tattoo parlor's grand re-opening was three months ago, and they'd been booked solid ever since. The new place outshone the old one, and his heart hurt because he still wished Carley was there to share in the success with him.

Fuck! Pull it together, man!

"Damn right. The world-wide attention doesn't hurt, either." Carson snorted.

Before the fire, Blank Canvas had hit the big-time, and so had Toby and his team, thanks to Minnesota Ink and Metal, an up-and-coming TV show about alternative lifestyles. Reality TV was at an all-time high, and he figured, why not milk that shit while he could? It was all thanks to his cousin. Ash was the lead singer of the popular rock band Love the Sinner, and he only went to them for ink whenever he got the itch for more art. Word spread after one MTV interview where the host had mentioned wanting body art of his own, and good ol' cousin Ash had put them up on the map by endorsing them to the world. It wasn't long after that the show began.

His life shifted quickly in a different direction. After Blank Canvas burned to the ground, he'd made some big changes: a new shop, a new name, and a new him. He'd crawled out from the gutter of grief and re-invented his life. That included not renewing his contract with the television network, but did his group of fans care? Nope. Business was booming, and he couldn't care less if his success peaked because most of the people who sought him out were hoping to catch a glimpse of the infamous Ash Harris or his brothers in the band. Toby knew he was damn good at what he did, and so were his employees, because he'd handpicked some of the best himself.

He loved what he did, period.

"You're fucking right, it doesn't." Toby smirked. "Busy days, good coin, and an endless supply of numbers to keep me company during the night."

"Speaking of pussy," Carson chuckled, "I'm heading over to Fanny's for a bite and a couple

11

drinks to unwind. You coming with?"

"Hell, yeah."

Fanny's was a local pub down the road. It was close enough to walk over. It was cozy, the beer was cheap, and the owner used to be an old neighbor, so he liked to help keep them in business. It hadn't hurt that Fanny herself was like a second mother to him, either. "Why not?" He shrugged. "I could use a couple drinks." Truth was he needed them. He was still having trouble sleeping. It'd been almost two years since his loss, and every time he closed his eyes, Carley's lifeless image still haunted him. If only he'd died with her that horrible night, maybe he'd be at peace. He shook his head. It wasn't that he was suicidal, per se. He was just tired as fuck. His brain didn't have an off switch, and he needed a little something to numb the memories. "The women? We'll see how it goes."

"Whatever you say, bro." His friend chuckled and led the way.

The pub looked like a local hole-in-the-wall from the outside in, but it was so much more, and it wasn't just because he was biased to it, either. It was just the way it was. Anyone who walked through the door came back again. Fanny's was notorious for its great food, cheap drinks, and hospitality. The moment he sat his ass down, he felt like he was home.

A mix of rock played in the background as he took his first sip of beer, and he smiled as he watched one of his most favorite people in the world approach him.

"Hey, sugar." The proprietor gave him a big hug

and smiled wide. "My day just got brighter now that you're both here." She turned to give Carson equal attention.

"Thanks, Mamma Deuce," they chorused, and Toby winked. Fanny and her husband were like family, and since some medical problems resulted in them not being able to have children of their own, they had sort of adopted him and his crew as surrogates.

Family didn't always have to be blood, and apart from Ash and maybe a handful of others, he'd withdrawn from those who were blood-related years ago. They were just too fucked up, and unfortunately, he had the pain of knowing it all too well. It didn't hurt that it was also easier to close himself off to keep from allowing anyone to get too close. Emotions sucked, and there was just no way in hell he'd allow himself to feel that kind of pain again.

Been there, done that, and could write the damn book.

There were still a select few who still gave a damn about him, no matter how much he'd tried to push them away. And thank fuck for that because it took a special kind of twisted to be a permanent part of his world. Hence the birth of his new shop and the name that came along with it. It suited them perfectly, every damned one of them.

"Oh, stop it." Fanny guffawed and waved them off. Toby knew she secretly loved their little pet name for her, though. Her eyes lit up every time, and like clockwork, it immediately followed her acting on those motherly instincts of hers. "I love

13

ya, Lord knows I do. Now, what can I get you?"

"The usual for me." Carson took a swig of his beer and surveyed the inventory of women as he looked around the bar.

Mamma Deuce nodded at his friend in response and arched a brow when Toby answered with, "Not hungry."

"Not good enough," she challenged. "You gotta eat, Tob, and since you're being so stubborn, it'll be whatever I bring you."

"Figures." He smirked and shook his head.

She walked away with a shout out of, "Tough love, Sugar, you know you love it."

Truthfully, if it wasn't for Fanny, he probably wouldn't eat at all. So yeah, it was kind of nice having someone look out for him once in awhile. Not that he'd ever admit that out loud.

***

"How can you eat that shit without getting severe heartburn, man?"

Carson discarded another chicken bone and licked the hot sauce from his fingers with a shrug. "Abs of steel, bro. You done with that?"

"I am now." He pushed the remainder of his meatloaf sandwich toward him with a grimace. "Enjoy."

"Fucking right, I will," his friend said around a mouthful, and Toby had just enough time to signal the bartender for another drink before they were interrupted by five feet, seven inches of soft, deliciously tempting female company. The night was looking up.

"Oh my God. Toby James? I've been coming here the last couple of weeks hoping to run into you. Can I have your autograph?" The blonde bombshell lowered the top half of her shirt to expose a supple amount of cleavage and handed him a marker.

Nice!

"You lucky bastard," the bottomless pit beside him muttered good naturedly, and the boobs that currently distracted him suddenly moved Carson's way for a second.

"Oh, don't worry. There's always room for you too," the nameless broad purred, and he arched a brow in momentary shock as she lifted her already barely there skirt to expose her thigh until she hit her panty line.

Skimpy and see through. Interesting.

"I'd say we both are." He popped the top of the marker off and signaled with his finger for her to come closer. "So, what's your name honey?"

"Candy."

Toby tried to cover the snort that came out. Shit, it was too easy and totally cliché. Miss Blonde, bright, and about to be fucked seemed interested, so what did he care? "Pretty name for such a beautiful girl." His thumb grazed the top of her tit just at the seam as he finished writing his name. He sat back. "Now that you've found me, what are your plans?"

"Well, I-I…" It was kind of cute the way she stuttered.

"It's been a long day, honey. Why don't you join us for a drink, and if you're up for it after, we can bring the party back to my place?"

"You wouldn't happen to have a friend around, would you? Or perhaps your comment of, 'there's always room for you,' means you're up for both of our company tonight, hm?" Carson interrupted and got straight to the point. They were both there looking to get laid, and if she wanted an out, now would be the time to take it. Did he care if she had a friend? Not particularly. It wasn't the first time he'd had to share and probably wouldn't be the last.

Candy jumped at the chance, and any nervousness she'd once had vanished instantly. "Well, I was supposed to meet a couple girlfriends here tonight, but I'm feeling selfish now. So what do you say we skip the drink and escape before they get here?" She pressed herself between both men and slid an arm through each one of theirs to get them moving. "I'm a bigger fan than they are anyway, and trust me when I say I can handle the both of you just fine."

"You sure? The more the merrier. Carson and I would be more than happy to have your friends join us, too." Toby shrugged, threw a few bills down for Fanny, which would cover everything plus a tip, and faced them again, ready to go.

"Very. Let's go." Candy tugged them forward, and both men chuckled. Their blonde plaything was eager for them and apparently wasn't into sharing with her friends tonight.

Toby's spacious studio apartment was above the shop just a few blocks away, and it took them no time at all to get there. Screw letting her look around, though. As soon as his door opened, he captured Candy's lips and began to undress her. That left Carson to close it behind them before he jumped into the action. They were a mixture of limbs, tongues, and teeth. Discarded clothing was being thrown across the place as they walked her backward until her legs hit the bed and Toby gently lowered her down. "You ready for this, sweetheart?"

"Hell, yes," Candy hissed. Her breath was laboured with need, and it gave them both a nice view of her bared breasts. His mouth began to water, and Toby's cock was so hard he ached.

"Whoa!" Carson chuckled as she pounced, pulling Toby on top of her again to feast on his mouth. "Slow down, babe. We've got all night." He watched while discarding his clothes before Toby pulled himself back from her to do the same.

This chick was on fire for them, and thank fuck because Toby really needed this, and now it was time to make her scream. Toby gripped the base of his cock and pumped himself a couple of times, enjoying the show. She writhed for his buddy as he trailed his mouth down her throat to her chest and stopped to pay extra attention to those luscious mounds.

Shit! So hot.

His control was wavering, and his cock slapped against his flat stomach when he let it go so he could grip her hips, pull her toward the edge of the bed, and spread her legs. Her pussy glistened with arousal, and Toby groaned at the sight of the smooth swollen lips and shiny pink center, which he suddenly needed to taste. He dropped to his knees and kissed, nipped, and licked his way up her thighs, purposely taking his time to drive her wild. But it worked even better the moment he took his first lick to her core from ass to clit and back again. He licked, flicked, sucked, and tongue-fucked her into oblivion. It was a part of sex he truly enjoyed, and he was so caught up in it that it took him a minute to realize he was being spoken to.

"Please tell me she tastes as good as she looks."

Toby's mouth glistened as he pulled back to smirk at his friend. "I do love my pussy." He shrugged, and Candy groaned with a plea.

"Please?"

"Please what, baby?" Carson chuckled. "Tell us what you want."

"Ugh," she writhed. "I want somebody to put their mouth back on my cunt so I can come. I'm so fucking close. Then I want to be fucked hard and fast, pounded so good I can see stars, then I want to taste one of you or both. Okay?"

"Is that all?" Toby winked and began to toy with her clit again, but with his fingers this time, and she moaned so loudly, he could feel her vibrate.

"Please?" she begged.

"Fuck, yeah. Switch places with me, dude. It's my turn to mouth fuck that sweet pussy." His buddy leaped off the bed to replace him. Carson got to work between her legs while Toby fisted his hands in her long blonde hair and feasted on her mouth, made her taste herself, and it was good.

Candy writhed and screamed in ecstasy within minutes, and now it was their turn. Carson quickly suited up with a condom, got her on all fours, and fucked her like she'd asked them to. Toby stood in front of her and tapped her mouth with the tip of his dick for the taste of him she'd practically begged for. The moment those soft lips and the delectable heat of her luscious mouth surrounded him, he was lost, and he knew without a doubt tonight would be a good night...to forget.

Chapter Three

HARLOW

"Hey, you." Harlow smiled with warmth as her friend Calista stood to embrace her. "I'm so glad I could talk you into coming."

"I know, and I'm sorry." Harlow bit her lip and scrunched her nose. "I've been hiding out like a hermit, and I need to re-learn how to join the living once in awhile." She spent most of her time alone at home or concentrating on work. Which meant she didn't get out to socialize much. When Calista called to meet for appetizers and a few drinks at a new restaurant around the corner from her, she figured, why not? If it came to be too much to handle, she was within walking distance to her safe haven, which was home.

The restaurant was a lot bigger than it looked from the outside. It had a modern look to it, with its polished black floors, chrome stools, and granite table tops. Clearly trendy and popular so far, judging by how packed it was, too.

"Ah, baby steps. And this is a great way to start, right?" Calista squeezed her hand and took a seat. "All work and no play makes a dreary existence. It's nice to see a little of the old you beginning to come out."

She nodded and shifted in her seat. "O-oh, hello?"

"Harlow Ross, meet Melody Tyler. Mel, Harlow." Her friend waved between the two of them and smiled.

"Harlow Ross? No eff'n way."

"The one and only." Harlow laughed nervously. It still fazed her how some people reacted to meeting her. The enthusiasm was flattering, but it was hard to get used to. She was treated as somewhat of a local celebrity. At least by women; the men, not so much. But that was her target audience anyway. "It's a pleasure to meet you."

"Likewise, and might I just say, I'm a total fan of your column in *Twin City Women's Magazine*. It's downright hilarious sometimes."

Okay, and how am I supposed to respond to that?

"Um, thanks—I think."

"Don't mention it."

Calista shook her head and looked amused. "I met Mel a few months back when I got this done." She lifted the sleeve of her shirt to expose the phoenix she'd had tattooed on her inner forearm. "Her brother, who did the tattoo, was an incorrigible flirt, and although he's harmless, Mel here got him to stop by cracking jokes. It was a riot."

"Carson's a great guy, but he chases anything in

21

a skirt." Mel rolled her eyes. "Sometimes he can come off a little strong, so what's a little playful banter between siblings when the outcome results in a few laughs and a bit of fun?"

"I agree."

"Callie tells me you were thinking about getting some ink for yourself."

Harlow had a glass of water in hand and was mid-sip before she began to choke. "Sorry, wrong hole." She wheezed and arched a brow toward her friend after she finished her bout of coughing and got it under control. She'd always been kind of awkward, especially in front of new people, and it was showing. "Yeah, I guess. I've been thinking about it for a while. Picked out a design so I can cover the scars, eventually, but I haven't made the leap to do it yet."

"Oh, come on, Har. I know you're still holding on, and the scars are some twisted way of reminding you…"

"Yes, Calista, they remind me that life is precious, and it can be ripped away at any second," she snapped, looked away, then took a deep breath to push the emotions back down. The anger, hurt, and the "what if's" would always be a part of her, and suddenly, the restaurant seemed like it was closing in on them.

Okay, deep breath in, one huge breath out, and repeat. Deep breathe in, and…out.

"I-I'm sorry."

"No, I am, honey." Calista sighed. "You talk about your design, and it sounds beautiful. It also has a lot of meaning for you. Why not take something bad and turn it into something pretty?"

"Which is why I'm here." Melody cleared her throat and blushed. "I can't imagine what you went through, and I'm sorry for your loss. I can't express how much, but I work at Misfit, and I'd be glad to hook you up."

A few years ago, four to be exact, Harlow had been in a major car accident, which resulted in the death of her then two-year-old daughter, Lily. About a year after it happened, and a change in career later, she'd opened up about it through her column. It was old news, and anyone who was a fan knew what happened and of her loss.

"Drunk Driver Jackknifes Semi Across State Highway Totalling Volkswagen Jetta. One Dead, One in Serious Condition," the headlines had read. The humongous truck had swerved and clipped her car just before the back end of the tractor trailer skidded sideways, narrowly missing them when it rolled over. She had no time to react to being run off the road. One minute she'd been checking the rear-view mirror to see her precious little angel sleeping in her car seat. The next thing she knew, she'd awakened heavily sedated in the hospital a few days later. Eventually, the doctor had told her she'd had to be cut out of her car, Lily had died painlessly upon impact, and Harlow was lucky to be alive.

Back to the present, Harlow, come on! Calista's talking to you.

"They're amazingly talented." Her friend beamed, completely oblivious to Harlow's internal struggle. "And they used to have that TV show.

You know the one, Blank Canvas Tattoo."

"You're a tattoo artist?" she asked Melody. She'd heard of the show but was too ashamed to admit she hadn't watched it and didn't want to offend anyone. She kept quiet about that fact. Yet the change of topic was nice to keep them from talking about her accident. Such a long time ago, yet it sometimes felt like yesterday.

She shivered.

"Not exactly. I'm actually their piercer." Mel winked. "But the guys are the best at what they do, and because you have an in, mainly me," she chuckled, "you won't have to go on the wait list for an appointment. I can get you in probably as early as next week."

"Seriously, there's a waiting list for tattoo shops?" Harlow didn't have much knowledge or experience in the tattoo business, but they'd piqued her curiosity.

Maybe I should just check the place out and see what happens. I always said I'd do this eventually, anyway.

She chewed her bottom lip and pondered on it.

"Thanks to the show and the fact that we're tied to Love the Sinner, we book up pretty fast." Melody shrugged. "Yeah, there are shops with wait lists. Not many can take walk-ins nowadays. People just show up, let us know what they want and where they want it, and we set an appointment at a different time. Before you make up your mind, why don't you stop by and check the place out first?"

"Okay, wait a minute," Harlow said. "As in the band? Are you serious?" She was having a fangirl moment suddenly. Her head was kind of everywhere now, though. "Oh my god. I love listening to them, and their single 'Sinister' is my new favorite." The other two women laughed at her and shook their heads in affirmation as she hummed the chorus.

"One and the same. The guys are a great bunch, and the shop's owner is related to their lead singer. What do you say? Meet me at Misfit next Friday at six? I'll show you around, and we can go grab a bite to eat afterward."

"Count me in," Calista exclaimed. "I can meet you two at Fanny's around seven. It'll give me time to get home from work and change."

Her heart raced as she tried to make up her mind. It'd been so long since she'd done something this impulsive. Not since before…

She shuddered and shook the thought away. "Sure. Why not. Friday at six. I think I can handle that."

"Oh!" Calista squealed with excitement and jumped up from her chair to give Harlow another hug. "You won't regret this. Now let's celebrate with a round of drinks."

Chapter Four

TOBY

Oh, fuck me!

He'd seen a lot of hot ass in his lifetime, but this chick was a fucking ten and then some. He couldn't help but gravitate toward the front to get a closer look. She had thick, long, brown hair almost down to her butt, a cute hourglass figure, flat stomach, perky tits, and a firm, round ass, from what he could see of her, anyway. He was rewarded with a side view of her now.

"Can I help you?" his receptionist, Dee, asked.

"I hope so." Ms. Hottie smirked. "I'm here to see Melody Tyler."

Mel, huh? Well, well, well. Somebody's been holding out on us.

"She's in with a client. Is she expecting you?"

"She is." The brunette bombshell looked to her watch and back up again. "Can you please let her know Harlow is here?"

"The Twin City chick?" Dee smiled.

Okay, what the fuck? I'm missing something here.

Hottie Harlow chuckled, and it went straight to his cock.

"Guilty." She bit her lip. "It's nice to meet you, uh…"

"Name's Diamond Rae, but I prefer Dee, and might I say, I totally admire what you do. You're an inspiration, honey. Have yourself a seat, and I'll see if I can get Mel to hurry it up."

"Um, thank you." She blushed.

Dee turned around and ran smack into him. "Oh, hey, Tob." She winked on her way by. "I'll only be a minute."

Toby nodded then leaned against the front counter. "Haven't seen you around before. Are you a friend of Mel's?" he asked as if he hadn't already heard.

Yep, the face is as hot as the rest.

The thought tugged at his heart, and he resisted the urge to rub his chest. She was that striking. Heart-shaped face, big, green, doe eyes, a small pert nose, and very luscious lips he could picture himself nibbling on.

"I guess, yeah," she answered with a shrug. "Mel's great. We went out the other night with a mutual friend and made plans to meet up tonight, and here I am."

"You getting pierced?" He looked at her chest and imagined tugging on a nip piercing with his mouth and laving it with his tongue for a taste. Toby shifted as the crotch of his pants grew uncomfortably snug.

27

Shit!

"No." She chuckled, as if the thought might be absurd. "I'm trying to gain enough courage to actually go through with getting a tattoo. It's been a long time coming, and Mel thought it might be a good idea to come in to check things out here first before heading out." She looked around. "I thought it would be much busier."

Now, that I can help with.

"It usually is." Toby chuckled. "My guy Carson's in with a client, Mel's with someone right now, and I'm waiting on my next appointment. We've been pretty steady, so much so that I'm looking to hire on more artists to meet the demand."

"I'm sorry I didn't mean to imply—what I mean is Mel told me about the wait list, and I clearly know nothing about the tattoo industry."

"It's all good, sweetheart." He shrugged. "What were you looking to get and where?"

"A skull with a long vine of flowers going through it to represent life and death intertwined." She took a deep breath. "I'd like it to be shaded in black and white, but I want color on the floral part to make it stand out. I'm not sure if my description is doing justice to what I have pictured in my head, but I want the branch-like vine to start at the top like a halo. It'll go through the skull and then drape down my side into a bouquet." Harlow walked closer to him. She turned to her side and lifted her right arm while her left hand pointed from under her breast right down past her ribs and ended at her hip.

Toby nodded and knew it was something he could do easily. "The ribs can be a bitch to cover, but I can see it. Picture your tattoo in my head. You know what type of flowers you want?"

"Yeah, I'd like a mixture. A pink carnation to start with. It's the traditional death flower, but I think they're pretty. Then maybe a lily, an orchid, a rose or two, stuff like that. Definitely need the lily to stand out. That's important. You know, pretty." She made cute little hand gestures while she spoke, and it left him smiling.

"You're going big."

Obviously, dumb ass. Way to state the obvious.

"It'll have to be big to cover the scars." Her eyes widened, and her hand flew to her lips as if she didn't mean to say that part out loud yet.

"Scars?"

"From an accident." Harlow sighed. "Car accident a few years back. Got cut up pretty badly, and, well…" She shrugged and kept it vague on purpose. "The scars are the worst on my side here."

"I get it." He nodded.

Scars?

Hell, he had a few of those, thanks to some of the burns he'd sustained when the old place had burned down. Toby suppressed the shudder that usually came after thinking about the fire and continued. "Can I see what we might be dealing with here?"

"You want me to lift my shirt?" She stared at him, incredulous. "Right this minute? Seriously?"

"Well, yeah, there's nobody around, and I promise to keep you covered." He smirked and walked around the counter to the waiting area to take a closer look. "Certain scars can be hard to cover up. Wouldn't you like to know if it can be done or not?"

"I guess so." She eyed him suspiciously. "What exactly are your credentials? For all I know, you could be some random guy who walked into this place. I don't even know your name."

"Good one." He chuckled and held out his hand for her. "Toby James at your service. I've been tattooing for over a decade, and I also own this place, but thanks for the laugh."

"Oh." Her eyes widened when he reached over the counter to hand her his business card, and she smiled. "Foot meet mouth. I'm Harlow Ross. It's nice to meet you."

"Yeah." He nodded to her and swallowed hard. "Come on back for a sec. It'll give you more privacy. Mel will be a few more minutes, anyway." Toby led her past the counter, into his new office space, and shut the door. "You know it's not every day I meet someone who doesn't already know who I am."

"I'm sorry?" Harlow looked adorably confused.

"The show and Ash made me and the shop somewhat of a celebrity around here. You never watched?"

"Guilty." She blushed. "I've been busy with my career the last couple of years, and I don't really watch much television. I'd rather read." Harlow cleared her throat. "Now about the tattoo…"

"Right. By all means, be my guest." They were back there so he could see the scar tissue he'd be covering up, after all. He'd already decided it'd be him that'd be touching her skin, marking her with his art, for her very first time. He'd make the time to pop this woman's tattoo cherry any day. Toby smirked as she lifted the side of her shirt for him. He really did need to check out the area to see how bad the skin was. He also needed to see how the tatt she wanted would fit with the shape of her body, if she went through with it. It also didn't hurt that she was somebody he wouldn't mind getting naked with, either. It gave him the opportunity to see more skin. There was something about her that intrigued him more than his usual one- or two-night distractions had.

Get your head out of your ass, dipshit. She's a potential client, and you might want a few rounds with her in the sheets, nothing more. Fucking concentrate!

"Well?" Her questioning look and raised eyebrow brought him out of his own thoughts as he studied the area in question.

Her skin looked smooth and incredibly soft, except for the damaged skin tissue that began from the side of her breast and ran down the length of ribs. A thin line of white slightly puckered out from her undamaged areas. Then it broke apart, curved toward her flat stomach, and she had three smaller-looking scars from belly to hip. Although smaller in diameter, the lower ones looked rougher, as if they'd had a much harder time healing. Without thinking about it, he traced them with his fingers, and it felt like a spark ignited. An electric current passed between them, and while Harlow gasped, he gritted his teeth to keep from growling. Whatever remained of his blood left the top part of him and headed south, just when he thought he couldn't possibly get any harder for her. He needed to get laid again, obviously.

Toby quickly stepped away and took a deep breath. "Good news is I think this is completely doable. I can spread out the flower part on the bottom to cover what you want, but they'll still be there. You get me? Cover-ups can be tricky, and the scars will be camouflaged but…"

"I get it." She held up her hands, and her shirt fell back into place. "And thank you. I'm just trying to make something horrible into something a little less ugly. They're a part of me now, a reminder to never forget."

He watched her look away, and he almost groaned as soon as he heard the voices down the hall coming closer. His time with her seemed to be coming to an end, for now. Dee was coming back with Carson and his client following close behind. He could hear them walk past. He quickly grabbed a piece of paper and asked if he could trace the area and mark an X along the length and the scarred parts for the sketch. When she agreed, he did so quickly and stepped back again. "This way, it'll be easier to make the design to cover up the right spots." Toby opened the door and walked with her back to the lobby a minute or two later.

"I appreciate it. Thanks, again." Harlow extended her hand, but instead of taking it to shake, he decided to place a kiss on it. He winked, and she turned a pretty shade of red. A minute later, his six-thirty walked in, and the usual chaos began. He just hoped she didn't chicken out and they would have an opportunity to meet again. "It's been a pleasure, Harlow. I'll see you around."

"Sure." She graced him with a smile as he walked away. Toby could hear Carson giving the normal aftercare instruction spiel to his latest canvas and shook his head with amusement as he heard him spot Mel's new friend at the reception desk. He listened vaguely to his friend's lame-ass pickup line before entering his private workspace.

"Damn, I hope you know CPR, because baby, you've taken my breath away..."

"Carson Emery Tyler! You leave her alone," Mel barked on her way toward the front, and his appointment started on a good foot with a hearty laugh. He couldn't remember the last time he'd smiled so much. The sound of brother and sister bantering, the phone ringing, a hot girl, and someone sitting in his chair waiting for ink. It was his life, and he counted every blessing he had before the darkness took hold again.

Chapter Five

~Idiosyncratic (i.e., idiosyncrasy): Is an individualizing characteristic or quality often used to express eccentricity in a person or situation.~

HARLOW

"I know this is a little unorthodox, but I was wondering if you could take a look at this for me." They'd arrived at Fanny's and were waiting for Calista when Melody slid a folded piece of paper across the table.

"What's this?" She looked toward her new friend with curiosity and opened it up.

"I meant to send that through the appropriate channels at the magazine for you to reply, but I figured, since you're already here, I'd just hand it to you in person."

"Oh?" Now she was curious. Helping people was a passion, the reason for her psychology degree. Since the accident, she'd traded in her cushy office and scheduled hourly appointments for the ability to

34

work from home with flexible hours. She still helped people, but now she did it through her *Harlow Helps* advice column at the magazine. It wasn't glamorous, but she enjoyed herself. It paid the bills and made her quite popular with the female demographic from the ages of twenty through to fifty. "Mind if I take a quick look while we wait?"

"Be my guest."

Dear Harlow:

I have this friend who's more like family, really, and I'm worried about him. We'll call him Mr. Idiosyncratic.

A couple years ago, tragedy struck, and it hit us all pretty hard, especially him, when he lost the love of his life and his life's work in the same moment. For a while there, none of us were even sure he'd pull through it.

There was a horrible fire on the night he proposed to his girlfriend, and I fear he still blames himself for surviving when he couldn't save her. He was burned badly on his lower legs, suffered from smoke inhalation, and it was a long recovery process. Problem is, I think he's still stuck in the nightmare.

He's a shell of the man he once was, and he hides behind this tough guy persona and a parade of meaningless bimbos. He also works himself raw to escape feeling anything too emotionally painful. I realize this is something one doesn't get over very easily, if ever, but his fiancé would have wanted him to live life to its fullest. To move on, not to dwell on the bad, and instead remember the good times they'd shared. She was amazing like that.

I guess I just wish there was something more we could all do to help him.

Do you have any suggestions? I figure you might be able to relate.

Sincerely,

Worried About a Brother

"He's lucky to have you." Harlow wiped a stray tear and looked away. She normally didn't get emotional over her work. She'd learned the hard way to detach herself from it, but there was something in this message that hit close to home. "But why use idiosyncratic?"

"Because he's a one of a kind, and I didn't want to use his real name, for obvious reasons." She gestured to her letter and back again. "I've never talked to a shrink before. I highly doubt he has, either. Let's face it. He's a guy." Melody smirked. "But I'm taking a leap with you because I know you've experienced a big heap of grief yourself. It's not the same thing, but I read what happened to you in the paper, and after…"

"Please, say no more." She held up a hand to halt Melody from rehashing her own demons. It was not the time nor the place to go there, and instead, she managed to muster up a smile to pretend the subject didn't bother her as much as it did. Not that she was fooling anybody. Everyone was a work in progress, right? "Did you want me to add this to the column, or would you prefer to keep this between the two of us? It's a little heavier than the letters I usually get."

"You'd do that?"

Harlow shrugged. "Not normally, since I started at Twin City, but I can make an exception this time, if you'd like me to. I feel like you've gone out of your way for me with the whole tattoo business, and we hardly know each other yet. The offer is the least I can do."

"I wrote that fully thinking you'd add it, but if you could, I'd really appreciate the discretion. He'd be pissed if he knew I wrote that."

"He must be pretty special for you to care so much."

"He's my brother from another mother." Mel sighed. "He's pushed a lot of people away, and there are only a few of us he lets get close. He'd do the same for me, if the roles were reversed. He's special, but he's also ridiculously talented, hard-working, and caring, and I know he loves fiercely when he opens himself up. When the right kind of girl comes along once more, she'll be one lucky chick. I just want to see him happy again. Nothing wrong with that, right?"

"Absolutely. Nothing at all wrong with that." Harlow tucked the letter inside her purse. "Let me sleep on it, go over your letter again, and I'll give you a reply the next time we meet up. By the way, I really liked your tour today, and I've decided to brave the temptation. Think you can give me a call sometime tomorrow so we can set up an appointment for that tattoo?"

"Seriously? Hell, yeah. I'll check. Toby and Carson are both ridiculously talented. Do you have a preference between the two of 'em?"

"I'll take your word for it and go with whichever one you decide to book. Beggars can't be choosers, as the saying goes, and both men seemed completely competent in their abilities."

Melody's drink flew out of her mouth and nose, and her laugh turned into a bout of coughing while she tried to compose herself. "Competent, huh? I'll be sure to let them know you thought so."

"Hey, what'd I miss?" Calista shimmied in her seat and looked between the two of them. "Ooh, that looks good." She pointed to their drinks. "I want one, too."

"Ms. Helps here has decided to get that tattoo after tonight," Mel exclaimed while pointing toward Harlow, then she stood. "As for my drink, I'll get you one, too. The next round's on me. Then we'll order some food."

Callie squealed and squished her with a bear hug. "You're doing it. Finally! Way to go, Har. You'll see once you get one. You'll want another in no time."

"Uh, huh, we'll see." She smiled and felt elated.

Harlow Ross was completing a long-awaited goal in memory of her daughter. It was as if she was opening a new chapter in her life, and it was going to be a good one.

Chapter Six

HARLOW

Dear Mel:

Mr. Idiosyncratic has clearly been through a traumatic ordeal. And although I'm glad he survived, I am also truly sorry for the loss you all have suffered, from his injuries to the death of his loving fiancé. I hope you don't mind, but since this is between the two of us, I've decided to be a little more in-depth with my letter to you instead of the shorter responses I usually give in my column.

Grief varies from one person to another. Sometimes it takes one person longer to go through the grieving process, as we all deal with things differently. It's a part of what makes us unique as individuals, and it has varying factors, like how close we were to the person we're mourning...that kind of thing.

In our bereavement, we often move between stages before achieving a more peaceful acceptance of death, and many of us aren't afforded the luxury of doing so in a timely manner.

But remember, this is a very personal process and only a quick glimpse to help you understand and put into context what Mr. Idiosyncratic is probably facing.

Here are those steps:

1. Denial and Isolation: In my case, I used to pretend my daughter was on vacation with her grandparents and would walk through my door with them any minute because it was easier than the harsh reality that my baby was gone and would never be returning. You mentioned hearing about my situation, and this step is a natural reaction to rationalize overwhelming emotions.

2. Anger: Once the denial begins to fade, reality sets in, and its pain re-emerges fiercely. It's blindsiding, and we're vulnerable, so that hurt turns into anger. It may be aimed at ourselves, an inanimate object, strangers, our families, or even the one we lost for leaving us. Rationally speaking, we know it's not their fault. Emotionally, however, there can be resentment. It's then followed by guilt for feeling that way, and that makes us angry yet again with ourselves or with the situation itself.

3. _Bargaining:_ When we feel helpless, there's often a need to feel in control. That's when the should've, would've, could've, what-if's, or if-only's come in.

4. _Depression:_ Losing someone you love is a very stressful experience, from how the death occurred, to the cost of the funeral, and how we're going to survive afterwards. It's our preparation for the final goodbye. It can be hard to get past, and sometimes all we need is a good hug and someone to be there for us, even when we try our hardest to push them away. So it's good that he has you to stand by him.

5. _Acceptance:_ Unfortunately, not all of us get here. When a death is sudden or unexpected, some may never get through the anger or denial. Coping with loss is a very personal experience. The best thing is to be a comfort for your friend and to just be there when he needs you most.

Another thing to think about is the possibility of Posttraumatic Stress Disorder. PTSD is a mental illness that involves exposure to trauma involving death, the threat of it, or serious injury. Trauma, like the fire Mr. Idiosyncratic experienced, can cause the recovery period to last much longer. He may re-experience it through vivid nightmares, flashbacks, or with thoughts of the fire that come from out of nowhere. He may have trouble sleeping. He can experience anxiety, have a *hard time concentrating, or feel irritable. Some people even manage to feel numb or detached, which might explain all the "bimbo's" and crazy work habits, as you put it. But please note: not all traumatic experiences lead to PTSD, and I am in no way diagnosing anything by mentioning it. It could very well be a possibility, though, so keep it in mind.*

I know you said your friend might not be interested in therapy, but maybe one day he'll change his mind. There are several counselling services he may be interested in for the future, and there are also support groups, if that's a more comfortable route. If you'd like more information on that, I'd be happy to provide a list of resources for you.

What do I suggest, you ask? I suggest you continue to be supportive. Give him the options I've listed about the resources out there to help him cope and talk it out. Express your concerns and your worries and continually remind him that there are people who care about him, no matter what.

Life goes on, one way or another.

I wish I could be of more help to you, but there's no easy answer here. The only one who can truly make a serious mark on Mr. Idiosyncratic and his life is Mr. I, himself, and the people who love and support him.

Life is what you make of it, after all, and

I say he's very lucky to have you in it.
  Sincerely,
  Harlow

"Baby, Lucky Charms must be your favorite kind of cereal, cause you look magically delicious over here."

"Carson." Harlow smirked and quickly closed her laptop. "How are you today?"

"Now, that's a loaded question," he said, wiggling his eyebrows.

Harlow laughed.

"Hey, what's so funny?" He slid the chair across from her out, turned it around, and sat down so they were now at eye level.

"You have a way with words that always manages to make me smile or laugh. Tell me—do those lines actually ever work?"

"Sometimes." He winked. "And, if all else fails, it's always good to leave a woman smiling."

"Touché."

"Do you come here often?" He gestured around the small coffee shop and back again.

"I do, since it's in the general neighborhood from my apartment, but I normally don't tend to bring work with me." Her fingers tapped on the closed computer. "I haven't seen you around before. Is this your first time here?"

She loved Dark Java's homey atmosphere, from their comfortable cushioned chairs, to the free Wi-Fi, to their friendly service, to the vibrant colors on the walls. But what made it better was the fact that it was a diamond in the ruff. A place not everyone seemed to know about, but once they did, they were hooked. Not only was the coffee great but so was the food they served. Sometimes it was just nice to escape from the walls closing in on her at home. Working from there had its perks, but there were times when Harlow felt like she needed a fresh space, somewhere with more windows and sunlight and, well, people.

"I, uh, stayed with a friend last night, and I needed a little caffeine pick me up before heading to work." He shrugged, but she also noted the slight tint of red in his cheeks. She bit her lip to keep from laughing at him again, but he changed the subject anyway. "What exactly is it that you do?"

"I'm surprised your sister hasn't mentioned it already. I'm thinking she might be one of my biggest fans." That seemed to pique his curiosity. "I currently write for *Twin City Women's Magazine* as an advice columnist. It's quite rewarding, it pays the bills, and I like that I'm able to work from home."

"Oh, fuck. You're not *the* Harlow Helps chick, are you? Melody reads that stuff every day. She's hooked and makes sure there's a current issue at the shop to read between clients. She and Dee eat that shit up."

He looked a little guilty for his choice of words, and she decided to take pity on him. "I take it you're not a fan, then?" She chuckled and continued talking before he could answer. "No worries, Carson. I'm not offended. I'm glad the girls 'eat that shit up,' as you say. Women love the column, and men…well…" She shrugged, not exactly sure on how to finish that thought. "Let's just say, I'm happy my target audience enjoys it enough to keep me comfortably employed. It's flattering. I think the key is to be relatable. I try to personalize each of my replies to the specific reader who writes in, and sometimes, if I see fit, I'll even put in some of my own experiences."

He grunted. "Speaking of, you talk to Mel lately?"

"Not since yesterday. Why?" A couple weeks had gone by since their last outing, and she'd been able to squeeze Harlow into the schedule to get her long-awaited tattoo.

"Did she give you the appointment? Toby's scheduled you in on his time off as a special favor."

"He did what? You're not serious?" Her eyes widened, and truth be told, now she felt a little guilty.

"Yeah, don't worry about it," he said, as if that would appease the uneasiness she suddenly felt. "He likes you."

"I-uh, um…"

Carson got his mischievous gaze back while she stumbled for a reply. "Did you know I once heard kissing burns about three calories a minute? Feel like a workout before I leave here?" He puckered for her, and the effect worked, because she broke out into a fit of giggles.

"Where do you come up with this stuff?" she asked, but instead of answering, he just lifted her hand and gave her a quick peck.

"If it's any consolation, I like you too, sweetheart." He winked, rose from the chair, and parted with a quick, "But I seriously gotta go or I'll be late."

Rendered speechless by his quick parting from the table, Harlow watched him buy a cup of coffee and wave at her before he left.

With a shake of her head, she dug out her phone to dial Mel, who answered after the first ring.

"Hey, Chica. What's up?"

"Why didn't you tell me Toby would have to squeeze me in on his days off?"

Mel sighed. "He probably sees it as you doing him a favor. He works like a dog, and he'd be here anyway. So why not?"

"Are you sure? Because I'd hate to put him out." She gripped her phone tighter. "I feel sort of guilty."

"As if," Mel replied. "Girl, I don't know what was said between the two of you the other night, but he seems intrigued, happy even, and he wants to do it. Not sure if it's the design or you. Whatever the motivation, this is good for him, and he's already started on some ideas to show you. You wouldn't want to waste all that hard work, would you? Toby's a genius. I can't wait for your reaction when you see what he's come up with."

"Well, when you put it that way." Harlow smiled. "Just one more thing before I let you go. Are you free for lunch? I finished writing you a response regarding your letter, and I'd love to give it to you. My treat!"

"Damn right, I am. What time are you thinking?"

"One o'clock? I'll meet you at the shop."

"Sounds good to me. By the by, how did you know Toby's schedule anyway?"

"I ran into Carson this morning, and he let it slip."

"Figures," Mel mumbled. "My brother has a big mouth. Don't mind him."

"He certainly is a one of a kind, but I think that's a good thing." Harlow smirked.

"Meh, he's all right," Melody teased. "I've got to go for now. I'll see you soon, okay?"

Chapter Seven

HARLOW

Her experience this time was much different from the last. The moment she walked into the shop, it was packed. The phone was ringing. There was a line at reception and no available seating in the waiting area, where a small group of people looked through the stacks of portfolios available to them.

"Harlow!" Dee waved her over after putting someone on hold. "Come on back here."

Wow!

She made her way behind the counter. "Thanks."

"Mel's expecting you. Why don't you grab a coffee or something in the break room while you wait? It shouldn't be too long."

"Uh, where?"

"Down that hall. Second door to the right."

The moderate-sized room consisted of two plush reclining chairs facing a small flat screen mounted to the wall fully equipped with an Xbox, games, and controllers. A small kitchenette to the left contained a large fridge. Her eyes landed on the coffee machine, and she sighed, contented.

Mm, coffee.

She moved toward it, with the intention of making a cup, when she noticed the table on the opposite end of the room and the unknown man sitting there from the corner of her eye. "Oh?" She jumped and placed a hand to her chest. "I'm sorry. I didn't see you there."

Damn, Harlow. You should really start taking in your surroundings.

"I noticed." He smirked playfully. "By all means, carry on. Don't mind me."

She nodded and began to rummage through the cupboards to grab a mug. "Would you like a cup?" When she looked over again, he was immersed in the book in front of him.

"Nah, I'm good." He gestured toward the glass of water beside him and watched her approach with interest.

"I'm Harlow. It's nice to meet you, Mr.—?

"Parker. Rebel Parker."

She stretched out her hand to greet him, and they shook.

"What are you working on there?" She pointed to the paper he was writing on, coffee forgotten.

"This," he replied, "is just a doodle to kill time while I wait for Toby to come around, and this is my portfolio." His head tilted towards a large book beside him, and he shrugged.

"That's amazing," she said while staring in awe at the gothic-looking fairy drawing he was in the midst of sketching, blown away by its detail.

"Let's hope the boss feels the same way." Rebel chuckled. "Because I'm hoping to be the next artist hired here. Toby and I go way back, but you never know."

"Well, with that kind of talent, I don't see why you wouldn't be." She shook her head. "I'm getting my first tattoo soon, and I hope it'll look just as good as that does."

"I was beginning to wonder." His mouth tilted up as he studied her. "Are you a new hire too, by chance?"

"No." Her mouth twitched.

Now that's a laughable thought.

She didn't have an artistic bone in her body. Hell, the best she could draw was probably stick figures. "I'm here waiting for Melody, actually."

"Lucky Mel." He winked.

"Hey, Reb. I finally have a few minutes free if…" Toby stopped dead in the doorway and looked between the two at his table with a raised brow. "Harlow?"

"Toby." She stood. "If I'm in the way, I could just—"

"Absolutely not," the boss man said. "I'm glad to see you."

"You are?"

"Yeah." He strode toward her and gently grabbed her hand to hold it. "I have a sketch for you to look at."

Her mind went blank the moment his thumb started rubbing against her skin, and she gulped.

Is it me, or did the heat just go way up in here?

Good Lord. What's with this man and my reaction whenever he's around? This whole place is filled with hot guys. That's what's up. There's Toby, Carson, and now this Rebel guy. Damn, maybe I need to visit more often.

She cleared her throat. "I'd love to, but I can see you're busy." She gestured toward Rebel and back again.

Toby wasn't having any of it. He gently tilted her chin up, forcing her to look at him, and she was suddenly immersed in a Toby-filled fog. He was gorgeous, with dark brown hair, short on the sides and a little longer on top, giving it a messy but sexy look. His clear complexion had a naturally tanned look, thanks to what she assumed were either a Greek or Italian heritage. He had these stunning brown eyes so dark, they almost looked black, and they had a way of hypnotizing her to not look away whenever he came near.

Harlow sighed with longing as her eyes caressed their way down his physique. Broad shoulders and muscular arms filled with tattoos she wouldn't mind exploring at another time, a flat stomach she knew must have been rippled with a six pack, and a tapered waist encased in form-fitting jeans. He clearly worked out. The man was a huge mass of muscle and ink. It was a heady combination, and she couldn't remember the last time she'd been this attracted to a man. It had been so long. Toby cleared his throat to gain her attention again, and she could feel the heat hit her face. He'd obviously caught her ogling. The smirk he wore just proved it as he spoke. "There's no time like the present. Hey, Reb, can you give me a few more minutes?"

"Whatever you say, boss man." Rebel looked amused and dismissed them by continuing to draw.

"Great!" Toby tugged her out of the room and toward his work station. She hoped he was about to show her what he came up with based on her description from last time.

She knew she was right when Toby handed her the sketch.

"Oh, wow!" It was picture perfect, even better than she'd imagined, and she couldn't help a tear from escaping down her cheek before she quickly wiped it away. Toby had really made her life and death tattoo a reality, and she was in awe of it. The large skull was shaded in black and grey, just as she'd described, with the traditional death flower, aka carnation, flowing through it from top to bottom, its stem working as a halo on top. The flowers continued to flow from the bottom, and she loved the vibrant colors and that he focused on putting lilies into the mix. "Thank you." It came out quieter than she'd expected, so she cleared her throat.

"Hey, are you okay?" Her answer was muffled the moment his big arms wrapped around her and he pulled her close.

She just needed a minute and stood there enjoying the warmth of his hug. It was sort of nice to be embraced like this, and the soft beat of his heart against her ear was soothing.

He smells so good.

"I'm fine. Sorry." Harlow stepped back and laughed. "I'm speechless because it's perfect, but

I'm also a little embarrassed because of my reaction." She traced the image lovingly and tried to explain. "Thank you for this. It's better than I'd imagined, and she would have loved it, too."

He didn't look certain, though. "She?"

"My daughter. Her name was Lily." She traced the flowers again and focused on a calla lily in the center.

"Was?" Toby held her hand again. "What happened to her?"

"Car accident. A drunk driver hit us, and I made it, but she—she didn't." Her eyes left the tattoo sketch and landed on him again to gauge his reaction.

"Damn, Harlow. I'm so sorry." He nodded as if he understood and squeezed her hand in a show of support she really appreciated. Truthfully, he looked devastated for her, and she couldn't stand the sight because it would only bring her down into that dark place that she didn't have room for anymore.

It'd been a long, hard road to recovery, because not only had she lost her daughter, she'd almost lost her own life as well. With time, she was finally starting to get back to how she used to be before all the tragedy began, and Harlow desperately needed to stay there. Losing Lily wasn't something she'd ever get over. It'd be with her for the rest of her life, but she had to go on. Heck, life went on, and through the tragedy, she'd learned to embrace life one day at a time. One step at a time.

"I can see why the lilies were so important to add." He gestured toward the drawing and back.

"And it's perfect, so thank you again for

knowing exactly what I needed it to be." It was time for a subject change, and there was no better way than to put the focus back onto him. "You're amazingly talented. To go from my words to creating this is just—wow. I can't draw at all."

"Oh, come on. You can't be that bad." He smiled.

Harlow shook her head and chuckled. "I am. Trust me."

"You'll have to show me what you've got sometime, and I might be able to give you some pointers."

Her smile broadened. "Maybe I will."

"It's a date, then. How about we talk more at your appointment? You know, to finalize the details." Toby smirked at her, and she could feel her heart beat faster.

"Hey, boss man. You got my girl in here with you?" Mel peeked inside the door and smiled when she spotted the two of them together. "I've only got an hour, so we'd better get a move on."

"You got it." Harlow tightened her hold on his hand and squeezed back. "And Mr. James? Just so you know, I'm looking forward to it."

"Is that so?" Toby teased. He stretched his hand out as she stepped further away until they couldn't hold hands anymore and he was forced to release her.

She stopped in the doorway when they lost contact and winked after she waved goodbye.

***

55

"What was all of that about?" Mel hardly gave her a chance to sit down before she was on her. They'd gone to a little mom-and-pop diner down the road and managed to grab a booth by the window.

"What was what about?" Harlow avoided eye contact and decided to look at the menu.

"Don't play coy with me." Her friend chuckled. "There were some major sparks between the two of you in there." She rubbed her hands together with excitement.

"It was nothing much, really." Harlow put the menu down and bit her lip. "Okay, it was not nothing. The other night, I described what I was hoping for in a tattoo, and Toby nailed it. It's beautiful, even better than I imagined it could be, and I got a little emotional for a minute. Lily would have loved it, Mel, and I can't thank you enough for getting my foot in the door. You weren't kidding about how busy you all are over there. It was a mad house today."

"It's certainly entertaining. The men come in because they know we dish out quality work and a few were fans of the show. Most of the women, however, come hoping to catch the guys' attention or are hoping to catch a glimpse of Love the Sinner. Ash and the boys are in frequently when they're not touring, and if you think it was busy today, try showing up on a day those guys are in house. Last time we had to have the cops there to control the crowd outside." The waitress showed up to take their order, and once she was out of earshot, Mel continued. "I knew Toby would get it right. He's the best, but I am sorry it brought up so much for you. I can't even begin to imagine losing a child like you did. Want to talk about it?"

"Uh, no." She took a sip of water the waitress had dropped off and elaborated further. "I appreciate the offer, Melody. Really, I do, but I'd much rather just enjoy this lunch with you and give you this." She pushed an envelope toward her. "Grief is a passage that never ends, but it has a chance to change through stages, and it's up to us whether we accept them or not. I'd like to think I have. Losing my daughter was a hard road to go down, and it's something I'll never get over. But, at the same time, I'd like to think I'm stronger for it in a way. Many see grief as a weakness or a lack of faith, but I'd like to think it's the price you pay for loving someone, and it's worth the risk to do it. My heart will never be as whole as it was with Lily, but I also know she'd want me to be happy. Here I am, trying my best to lead by example and make my daughter proud by helping others because it's what I enjoy. I struggle sometimes, though, and speaking of—" She pointed to the letter in her friend's hand. "It sounds like your Mr. Idiosyncratic is having a hard time of it, too. He's very lucky to have you, and I hope this helps. If you'd like a list of resources, I can get one for you, and heck, if you think he'd be willing, I'd talk to him myself, if that's the route he'd be more comfortable with. Just let me know if there is anything more I can do, all right?"

"Will do. It's much appreciated." Mel lifted the sealed envelope with Harlow's reply before tucking it safely inside her bag. "I'll read this over and try to figure out the next step."

"Good idea." Their food came, and they spent the rest of their time idly chatting about random, less heartbreaking things, while they ate and made plans to call Calista for another night out soon to celebrate taking the leap again. Only this time, Harlow wanted Mel to invite Diamond, too.

Chapter Eight

Dear Harlow:

I confronted my boyfriend because I thought he was cheating. When I brought it up, he denied it at first. Later, he admitted to a onetime thing, and he promised he wouldn't do it again. I'm devastated, but I love him. What should I do?

~Confused in Minnesota~

*

Dear Confused:

It sounds self-explanatory to me. He denied it and told you it wouldn't happen again? I'd go with your gut. If there is no trust, there isn't much of a relationship to hold onto.

I wish you all the best,
Harlow.

***

TOBY

"You ready for this?"

He watched Harlow nod as he applied the stencil to her skin. This was it. She was taking a leap to pretty up her physical scars, and he was proud to be helping her out with that. He knew all too well how hard it was to deal with the death of someone you loved, and he admired her strength. "Okay, I'll need you to look in the mirror right there and you can let me know if the placement on your skin is right for you. Then we can get started."

"It really is quite big, isn't it?" She smiled and looked at it in awe through the reflection of the glass. "As I said, perfect, though." Harlow turned around and sat back on the chair. "Let's do this."

"You're a brave woman," Toby remarked, and he meant it in more ways than one. She was watching him as he slipped on gloves, removed the sterilized needle from its packaging, and set up. Harlow's skin was smooth and so soft to the touch. She was naked from the waist up except for her bra. She trembled slightly as he leaned in closer to start, and he felt like he needed to tread carefully and walk her through it, considering it was her first time. "I'll need you to lie back on your side for me and keep that arm away from the area we're working on, so with that in mind, position yourself in a way that makes you comfortable." He continued as she adjusted her position. "I won't lie and tell you this tickles, because it sure as hell doesn't. You're going to feel pain and discomfort. The ribs are especially sensitive. After about five or ten minutes, your endorphins should kick in, and it'll ease the feeling some, hopefully. If at any time you need a break, just say so and we can take five."

"Okay, how long do you think it'll take?" Harlow tucked her hands under her head to get comfortable, and it gave him just enough room to proceed.

"Two, maybe three hours. We won't overdo it this time. We'll just stick with the outline today. Let's give it some time to heal and schedule you back within a couple weeks. Then I'll finish it off with some shading and color."

"Sounds good to me." She took a deep breath in and out. "Thanks, Toby. I really mean it. You'll never know how much this means to me, especially with you fitting me in on your time off."

"People like you are the reason I do what I do. You make me feel like I'm making a difference, but I'm just an artist doing what I love. I'm honored, though."

"Right." She smiled.

The buzz of his tattoo gun filled the room, and it was music to his ears. He was in the zone and ready to get down to business. Harlow flinched and let out a hiss of pain the moment his needle penetrated her skin, but she was a trooper.

"What made you decide to go through with it?" Toby asked. There was nothing like a good distraction, so he tried to keep his clients talking. It was an effective way to make them feel more at ease. It was also a good way for him to subtly get to know her better.

"Long story short, Calista, my friend, came here to get some work done, and she talked about it non-stop. She was so pleased with the outcome. She's likeable and makes friends easily. I think it was Carson who did her tattoo, though." She smiled. "Mel overheard him flirting with Callie, and I guess after a bit of sibling banter and laughter, she struck up a friendship with Melody. She knew I wanted to get something to cover the scars and introduced me to Mel one night at dinner. She told me about this place, insisted I come have a look, and the rest is history."

"I guess you were impressed, then," Toby replied.

"You guessed right. This place is great, and so is everyone I've met so far. But if I'm going to be completely honest, it was you who helped me take this leap most of all. The moment I saw what you created, I was in love with it." She grunted as he kept working and listening. "I could picture it in my head. I described it, after all, but it didn't fully come together until I saw it on paper for the first time. I'm probably not even making sense, huh?"

"No, I get it." He chuckled. "I swear, my head swells every time I see you. I appreciate the compliments. Keep them coming."

"Right. I'll be sure to keep that in mind for the next time," she teased.

The buzzing continued, and he heard Harlow breathing heavily. "You're doing great. Be sure to let me know if you need a minute."

"I'm good."

"No doubt." He shook his head. "Tell me about your little girl." He could feel her body stiffen, but he wasn't sure if it was due to her physical discomfort or because he asked about her daughter.

Way to go, dipshit. Who wants to talk about hard shit? Ask about her daughter. She'll probably think about her death.

"Or not. Shit. Sorry. I shouldn't have brought her up."

He could feel the second her body relaxed for him, then she put him at ease. "No, it's okay, I guess. What is it you'd like to know?"

"Not sure. Anything you'd like to share."

"Okay, well, Lily Jane Ross was born September 19, 2012, and I fell in love with her before I even laid eyes on her. I swear, the moment I found out I was pregnant, I was overjoyed. I'd always wanted to become a mother. The first time I heard her heartbeat, my own heart swelled with excitement. It was miraculous. She was a whopping nine pounds, two ounces and absolutely perfect in my eyes. She was the sweetest. I swear it."

"Sounds like it," he said. "Big baby, too."

Harlow shrugged but didn't reply. She continued with her own descriptions. "She got that from her father's side, I think. He was about your height. Six-three or so, but I didn't know as much as I would've liked to about his side of the family. The moment I got pregnant, he wanted no part of it, but that's another story altogether." She paused. "I close my eyes, and I can still see her curly blonde hair, sparkling green eyes, and when she smiled, she had the cutest little dimple in her left cheek."

"Sounds like a beautiful memory to keep." Toby scooted his chair closer.

"A memory, yeah." She sniffed. "What I wouldn't give to have her be a reality again."

Toby gulped but didn't say a word. He knew exactly how she felt. The angst was in the air, thick with emotion, both hers and his combined. It was beginning to be too much, and he had to concentrate.

"Well, I was happy to do this for you. Now tell me what Harlow Ross is like."

"Oh God." She groaned. "Well, for one, I hate being put on the spot."

Toby chuckled. "Aren't you in the public eye, normally? You do write a popular column for Twin City, right?"

"I do, but it doesn't really work that way. Writing is a subtler way to get to know me. I choose what I'd like to share. But I love that it also allows me to get to know my readers as well when they write in. I mostly get to work from home, and when I do get recognized, it's usually through a mutual acquaintance. I'm not as big a celebrity as you are. Come on."

Call it a hunch, but he knew she was smiling for him. "Oh, you think so? If I recall, you didn't know who I was when we met," he teased.

"Yeah, but I also don't watch much television. If I'm not working, I'm escaping inside a book."

"You're so refreshing, Harlow Ross. Let's see what I've learned so far. You're, what, five-five, maybe a buck fifteen or twenty? Brunette, curvy in all the right places, sexy, and cute. You're also smart, have a great career you clearly enjoy, and good friends. You don't watch TV, but you like to read. You're career driven, a family woman, you love fiercely, and you're nice to talk to. Oh, and before today, you were a tattoo virgin. Am I missing anything?"

"Wow," she mumbled.

"And clearly humble." Toby smiled.

"You got all that from the few brief times I've run into you?"

"I pay attention. I'm good at reading people, too." He shrugged, wiped her skin with a paper towel, and leaned back to dip the needle in more ink. "I could tell you were a good one."

"I think that's the sweetest thing I've heard in a long time," she remarked. "Honest to God."

"Nothing sweet about me, but you want to think that way, knock yourself out." Toby grinned.

"Okay." She nodded. "So how about you tell me more about Toby James this time?"

Chapter Nine

HARLOW

"Not that interesting. Trust me," he replied.

"I find that hard to believe." She scrunched her face up and tried to breathe through the pain. It hurt like a bitch, but the result would be so worth it. Misfit Tattoo was not what she'd expected a tattoo parlor to be. She had pictured fat, hairy biker guys with beer bellies wearing too-small jeans that would show their asses anytime they bent over or sat down. She had pictured a dive building with questionable people who had piercings and mohawks and rainbow-colored hair. A total stereotype and cliché way of thinking and she was ashamed she'd thought that way.

Misfit was beautiful. A new construction building with blue walls covered in artwork, dark hardwood floors, a counter with a granite top, and a digital POS system. There was a big, red, neon sign that read **'BLANK CANVAS'** in the back. Mel had told her it was the sign from the old shop that burned down. They had a cool break room with a TV, a gaming console, and plush chairs. Leather seating adorned the lobby area for people who had to wait around. The tattooists were gorgeous, especially Toby. They all had amazing personalities and were extremely talented tattooists. She had been wrong on every account. Yes, there was ink, piercings, and colorful hair, but it was refreshing. Every client had privacy. It was exceptionally clean, and it was strictly professional at all times. She looked around the room and admired the posters, pictures, and signed memorabilia on the walls. "You described what you thought of me, so let's see if I can do the same for you."

"Be my guest," he replied.

"Okay." She was breathless for a second because of a particularly sore spot on her skin. "Toby James is a successful businessman who works hard and is passionate about what he does. You're engrossed in the art you create for others. You're a sentimental man, you have great friends and co-workers who care about you, and I have a feeling you love fiercely, as well. A family man too, perhaps? You work out regularly, from what I can tell about your physique. You're tall, big, and muscular. You have brown hair and the darkest eyes. They're quite nice to look at, I'll admit. Handsome, clearly, sexy as you put it, but I can also tell you're going through something big. Let's chalk it up to one lost soul recognizing another. How am I doing so far?"

"I'm impressed." Toby sounded amused. "Think I'm sexy, huh?"

"Is that all you got from what I said?" She rolled

her eyes.

Moving on!

"I like your posters. Is it all from Love the Sinner?"

"Yeah, Ash and I are tight."

"Mel was telling me Ash Harris was a relative of yours. They visit often?"

"He is, and when they can. Depends on the length of their tour and what new album they're working on." He sounded wary.

"They're a great band. Total fan over here."

"They all are," he said in a clipped tone, and she wondered if she offended him somehow.

"Everything okay?"

Toby sighed, and she could hear his chair slide back. He wiped at her skin again and went back to finishing the outline.

"Toby?"

"Look, you seem like a nice chick, so I'll give it to you straight. If you're a groupie looking for an in with the band, you'll have to get in line. Don't know when Ash is coming back, but I'm sure Mel will give you a heads-up anyway. Good luck with the crowd because it gets pretty crazy around here when the boys step in. Not in the habit of playing 'who gets to hook up with my cousin.' If that's your game, you're barking up the wrong tree. Ash has no trouble getting his own pussy. Never has. We clear?"

She could feel her whole body heat with both embarrassment and fury that he'd automatically make that assumption. Her? A groupie? It was laughable. She hadn't been on a date in over a year.

Hadn't gotten laid in almost five. But he wouldn't know that, so it was time to set the record straight.

She winced and clenched her jaw to keep her anger in check. "Have you ever heard the expression 'don't judge a book by its cover?'"

"Huh?"

"Okay, timeout for a second," she said.

Toby rolled back so she could sit up and look him in the eye.

"Heard the expression, have you?"

"Yeah, who hasn't?" he said, looking at her warily.

"Okay, well, I'm repeating it because you just made assumptions about me that were completely out of line. Here I am, laying here, having a conversation that you started, by the way. I'm not sure where it went wrong, but clearly it did. I liked your posters. They're cool, and I happen to be a fan of someone you're related to. It's not every day you meet someone with famous relatives. Their music is good. I listen, so sue me. I am not some groupie, nor will I ever be. I meet your cousin one day, great. I get an autograph. I have no interest in hooking up with him. I don't meet him, that's fine too. It's not something I'll lose sleep over."

"Babe." Toby shook his head.

"Babe? Babe!" She threw her hands up in the air, on the verge of giving up. "What kind of answer is that? I'm not sure what type of women you're used to, but FYI, I'm not one of them, Toby. I don't use people, I don't like to lie, and I definitely don't like to be classified in that category, so next time, just ask if I have a hidden agenda. Don't assume." She folded her arms across her chest.

"Careful there." Toby loosened her arms and held her hand. "I apologize for offending you, seriously. Women come in here all the time for Ash and try to cozy up to one of us for an intro, hoping to catch his eye. You're the first genuine woman I've seen in a long time who isn't like family to me. When you brought up Ash, I began to wonder if you were like all the rest. Glad to know you aren't."

"Are we almost done here?" She exhaled loudly and looked away.

"Halfway." His reply was automatic. He let go of her hand and reached up to cup the side of her face. "I'm sorry, Harlow. Forgive me?"

"Forgiven." She nodded. "What do you say we put on some music for the rest of it? Not sure I'm in the mood to talk anymore."

"Music, sure." Toby got up, plugged in his iPhone, and his cousin's latest song hit the speakers. It was back to business. She was halfway there, and the remaining time spent on the outline was silent, except for the buzz in the air and the low volume tunes she had requested.

Toby James was a beautifully complicated man, and she really wanted to figure him out.

Chapter Ten

HARLOW

"How'd it go?" Calista asked.

It had been a couple of days since her first tattoo session with Toby, and Harlow was at Fanny's with the girls to let loose. They were sharing some wings and having a few beers to unwind. "Good, I guess." She shrugged. "But it's so itchy. It's driving me nuts."

"Moisturizer," Dee commented.

Melody chimed in. "Keep putting lotion on the skin. Lots and lots of lotion, but no matter what, do not scratch, and for the love of God, leave the scabs alone. Wash with soap and water, then moisturize the hell out of that bitch."

Harlow pulled out a small bottle of Aveeno cream from her purse and smiled. "Don't leave home without it."

Callie laughed. "Good. Now get up and let's have a look. If it's itchy now, I'll even put some on for you, if you want."

Harlow sighed but decided, what the hell? They wanted to see it, so she'd get it over with now. She'd only be showing her midriff, not any of her lady bits. She looked around the place, and nobody seemed to be paying attention to them anyway, so she stood, lifted the side of her shirt, and lowered the top part of her jeans a couple of inches. "Toby said we'd be meeting up within the next couple of weeks to finish it. Last session was just the outline."

"Damn, girl. That's hot." Mel grinned.

Dee nodded in agreement. "Very nice."

"Oh, Har." Calista stood back to admire it. "It's amazing."

"I thought so, too." Harlow beamed. "Toby's talent has no limits."

"Don't tell him that." Dee snorted.

"Too late."

Well, shoot! Speak of the devil…

Harlow quickly righted her clothing and spun around at the sound of his deep timber. "Toby?" His name came out breathless, and she flinched.

Woman, pull yourself together.

Toby's grin was all teeth. He stepped forward and put his arm around her shoulders as they faced the group. "Complimenting me even when I'm not around? I like it." He winked at her and addressed the others, "This woman right here has officially become one of my favorite people."

Carson chuckled, and Rebel just shook his head, looking amused yet again at her expense.

"Get in line," Calista said. "She's been one of my favorites for years."

"Phoenix!" Carson cheered. "How's it going?"

"Phoenix?" Rebel arched a brow.

Calista rolled up her sleeve to show them the phoenix on her forearm. "Carson gave me this a little while back."

"Sure did." Carson moved around the table to step next to her friend. "Hey, baby. For some reason, I was feeling a little off today. But one look at you, and I'm definitely turned on now." He grinned, and Harlow busted out laughing.

"Knock it off." Mel grimaced. "You're going to make me sick."

"Okay, then." Rebel clapped his hands together. "I'm thirsty. Anyone need a top up?"

"I could use one," Dee said.

"You got it!" Rebel winked at her.

"Drinks for everyone," Toby remarked as he squeezed Harlow's shoulder before he stepped away. He looked her in the eye then said, "Be right back."

And she melted. Damn. That man was sex on legs, and he knew it too. She was in so much trouble.

***

TOBY

"What's up with you and Hottie Harlow?" Carson asked.

Toby, Reb, and Carson stood by the bar, waiting for Fanny to fill their drink orders.

"What's it to you?" Toby crossed his arms and

narrowed his eyes.

"Relax, bro. Just noticed you haven't been able to take your eyes off her is all. She's a nice piece. You don't want in, I'd be happy to give her a go."

"I would too, in a heartbeat." Rebel snorted. "But something tells me she's already been claimed." He smacked Toby's shoulder playfully and turned back to the bar.

"The hell you say." Carson looked at Rebel strangely, and it made Toby stiffen his posture. "Seriously, dude. Look at her. She may look like an angel, but I bet she fucks like the devil. It's the best of both worlds."

"Enough," Toby warned. "Harlow is off limits to both of you."

Carson chuckled. "Guess we're not sharing this one, huh?"

"What'd I just say?"

"I hear you." Carson put his hands up in surrender and took a step back. "Congratulations, man. It's about damn time."

"The fuck you on about?" Toby got in his face, and Rebel intervened.

"Nothing, Tob, he isn't going to mess with your girl, and neither am I. Just happy for you, man."

"Not my girl, but this one is different." He sighed as he tried to explain to them what he wasn't quite sure of himself yet. He raked his hands through his hair and gave up for the time being. Their drinks were up anyway, so it was time to make their way back to the table and to the woman who had him all tied up in knots.

Here goes nothing.

"Peace offering." Toby pulled the chair beside Harlow and got comfortable as he handed her a refill. He'd bought the whole table a round.

"For what?" She smiled and took his offering.

"I was an ass the other day." He took a chug of beer and winked. "Not often I admit that."

"I bet." When she smiled, he noticed her eyes had a sparkle to them. They were such a piercing shade of green, it was becoming his new favorite color.

"Friends then?" He held out his hand to shake hers, and she obliged.

"Friends," she repeated.

"What's this I hear about you being an ass?" Mel propped her elbows on the table and leaned forward.

"Shit!"

"Now you've done it." Harlow winked. She then answered Mel so he wouldn't have to. "At my appointment, we were having good conversation until about half way through the outline. I was remarking about the posters and memorabilia Toby had on his walls for Love the Sinner, mentioned I was a fan, and Toby not-so-politely assumed I was a groupie. Long story short, I set him straight, and he apologized and explained about most of the women who stop by the shop to get into Ash's pants."

She faced him and gave his arm a squeeze. "Thanks for the gesture, but no peace offering was necessary. I appreciate it, though."

"We never did get a chance to make plans. We were supposed to so I could check out your mad drawing skills, remember?"

"You can draw?" Carson asked her. Then he looked at Toby. "She can draw?"

"No." Harlow snickered. "Nothing more than a stick figure, maybe. I totally suck."

"We'll see." He smirked. "How about dinner Thursday? I'll check my calendar and figure out when I can fit you into the schedule so we can finish that tatt."

"You're on." She beamed, and he could feel it in his chest when she looked at him that way. He'd have to tread carefully with this one, otherwise it could be damaging to his heart. It was still filled with Carley, and he wasn't ready to let that go yet. Harlow was different, all right. She was the whole package.

A package that could be trouble if he wasn't careful.

So, cheers to friendship!

He took another big gulp of his beer.

Chapter Eleven

THREE YEARS EARLIER

In the Blink of An Eye
By Harlow Ross
January 2015 Issue

A few months ago, I was approached by this magazine with the chance to launch an advice/help column, and it came to me at an opportune time in my life. You see, I was looking for a change. I desperately needed one in my life, and I'll soon tell you why.

But first, I'd like to take an opportunity to announce how much I'm looking forward to getting to know you all as you get to know me before we get to all the heavy stuff I'm about to share.

So, for this column, my very first, I thought

I'd take the leap with something different from the typical advice columnist norm. I'm going to give you me.

I think it's important to establish a rapport as we go forward.

You ready?

Hi Readers, my name is Harlow Ross, and it's a pleasure to meet you all. I'm currently twenty-six, and I was born and raised in Fresno, California. I have a psychology degree from Stanford University, which I put to good use when I landed a job at St. Paul's Family Services in this great city shortly after graduation.

I come from a wonderful family. My parents have been happily married for the last thirty years. I have one sister who I adore, and I once had the most beautiful daughter in the world. She was my everything. Until one evening, in the blink of an eye, my whole world changed. Completely shattered, destroyed.

It was a nightmare that'll forever haunt me.

I'm not sure if any of you can recall reading about it, but about a year ago, almost to the day, I got hit by a drunk driver, and it cost me my life as I once knew it. I was critical, they tell me, yet I somehow survived my injuries. My two-year-old daughter, however, wasn't so lucky. My precious Lily was just gone. So, as I take a deep breath while I write this because it's still so hard, I'd like to honor her by telling you all a little about her.

I fell in love with my daughter before I ever laid eyes on her. I've always wanted to be a mother, and although Lily came into my life a bit sooner than I originally planned, she was my everything. The first time I heard her heartbeat was phenomenal. My own heart swelled with excitement. She was my miracle. I had her in the fall of 2013 at the healthy weight of nine pounds two ounces. She was perfect in my eyes, so sweet, really. I close my eyes and I can still see her smiling face, hear her giggle, and see her curly blonde hair, sparkling green eyes much like my own, and she had the cutest little dimple on her left cheek. Lily loved the outdoors, especially the swings at the park, and her favorite hobby was to color pretty pictures for our refrigerator. She was curious by nature and had questions for almost everything because everything seemed to fascinate her. I was honored to be her mother. I am honored still. So, for Lily, I continue to go on to the best of my ability because I know she'd want her mommy to be happy.

And helping people makes me happy, so here I am, making a change in my life at a time I feel good enough to try something new and exciting.

Welcome to Harlow Helps, everyone. It's the newest column here at Twin City Women's Magazine. I truly look forward to hearing from you all.

All my best,
Harlow

***

TOBY

Toby ran a hand down the front of his face and leaned back in his chair as he finished reading Harlow's first article from three years ago. It was an impulsive move to look her up online and read an article or two, but he couldn't help himself. He was all alone at home with nothing but his thoughts to occupy him, and she made him curious.

He took a big breath and exhaled heavily as he picked up his phone and debated whether it was a good time to call her. They'd made plans, and it was only right that he called to confirm. He thought about it, and well, it was the excuse he was going with.

He felt connected to Harlow somehow, probably because she understood his grief. What was wrong with making another friend? A hot, sexy, fucking gorgeous friend. Shit, it'd be so much easier if she didn't make him nervous because of how attracted he was to her.

You can do this, shit head. You loved Carley. Still do, right? Carley, Carley, Carley...Damn, baby. I miss you.

"Fuck me!" he growled. Toby stood up so fast his chair knocked over, and he began to pace. "Get a grip, dude." He threw his hands in the air and gripped his cell phone tighter. "Crazy ass, talkin' to yourself. Just make the call."

Before he could talk himself out of it, he dialed the number she had left at the shop and rubbed the back of his neck as it rang.

"Hello?"

"Hey, Harlow, it's Toby. I just wanted to make sure we were still on for tomorrow night."

"Dinner, right?" she said, and he could swear she was smiling as she said it, too. Don't ask him how. It was just a feeling.

"Yeah," he said. "I was hoping."

"Wouldn't miss it, then." She sounded happy, and it made his own mouth twitch just hearing it.

"Good to hear. There are no allergies I need to worry about, are there?"

"Not from me," she replied. "Where are you taking me? So I'll know what to wear."

"I was thinking Mecca's on Richfield. Shit, I hope you're not vegetarian."

"Ooh, nice, and nope. You're good once again. I totally love a good steak." She practically purred, and his dick twitched.

Shit!

"Toby?" She said his name like it was a question when he grew quiet for a minute.

"Still here." He sighed and rubbed the stubble

81

against his jaw. "It's getting late. I should probably go."

"Okay," she whispered, as if she sensed his inner dilemma. "I'll see you tomorrow, then."

"Tomorrow," he repeated. "Can you meet me at the shop around seven?"

"Sure. I look forward to it." He could hear her exhale on the other end. "Sweet dreams, Toby."

"I wish. Night, Harlow."

Fuck! Did I just say that out loud? I wish? Really?

Toby disconnected the call before she could say any more and tossed the phone onto his coffee table. Sleep evaded him, and he didn't feel like going out. He decided to do the next best thing instead by picking up his sketch pad and letting his pencil take control. With thoughts of a certain hottie columnist-slash-psychologist-slash-kindred spirit on his mind, it was no wonder the picture turned out to be her in the end.

He was fucked. Well and truly fucked.

Chapter Twelve

HARLOW

Each season had its own distinct characteristics, and because she lived in the Upper Midwest, they had such a wide variety of weather from one extreme to another. The winters were freezing, the fall and spring were damp, and the summers were hot, period. There seemed to be no in between.

The sun shone brightly on this mid-July evening, and Harlow had to place a hand on her forehead to block out its rays. She opened her car door and stepped out.

Here goes nothing.

She stood on the asphalt parking lot in front of Misfit, ready to meet Toby. Her nerves were starting to get the best of her, and she took a deep breath to settle them as she shut the door behind her. At the click of a button, her car beeped to indicate the locks had engaged. She reached into her purse to grab her shades and put them on. This felt so much like a date, and she hadn't been on one of those in God knew how long. She honestly couldn't remember, but she also knew deep down that Toby probably didn't feel the same way. This was business to him. Mostly. Probably. Maybe.

"Harlow!"

She started and placed a hand to her chest.

"Up here, babe." She looked to see Toby waving from the side of the building, and she headed toward him.

"Hey, you." She smiled when she reached the stairs.

"Come on up." He gestured for her to follow him as he disappeared behind a door she never noticed before now. Not that she'd been to Misfit very often.

"You live here too?" she asked.

The view of the spacious loft apartment above the shop was unexpected, but she had to admit, it was a cool space to be in. It was bright and airy with several large industrial windows. There were light-colored, hardwood floors throughout, and it was so open she could pretty much see everything all at once. There, in the far-right corner, was a large, plush-looking, king-sized bed. Yep, leave it to her to zoom in on his bedroom right from the get-go. She held back a groan and looked around. The opposite end of the room held a small but modern kitchen with white granite counter tops, dark grey cupboards, stainless steel appliances which included a gas stove. A small, two-seater wooden table was nearby, followed by a cozy living room. Classic artwork decorated his walls, which she assumed was his own work, and there were a few personal pictures scattered about.

"Yeah. Pretty convenient, huh?" Toby peeked his head out from behind the only other door in the place, so she guessed it was the bathroom.

"I like it." She gave him a slight nod of agreement and rubbed nervous hands down the sides of her dress as if she were trying to smooth out some non-existent wrinkles in the fabric. She took a deep breath and straightened her posture to exude confidence, at least outwardly.

Toby walked out of the bathroom and smiled. "Sorry about that. I spilled some coffee earlier, so I needed a quick change before we go." He looked her up and down appreciatively. "You look beautiful."

He reached out to touch her hair, curled a strand of it around his finger, and let go. "I've never seen it done up before."

She shrugged. Her hair was pinned up loosely to get it off her shoulders, and a few strands were left loose in the front. "I don't get out much. I guess I got carried away and dressed up." She gestured to her summer dress and her hair.

"I'm flattered. Thank you." Toby winked, and she blushed. He grabbed a set of keys from the coffee table and placed his hand on her lower back to guide her out. "I figured you could leave your ride here and we'd take my Jeep."

"S-sure." As they descended the stairs, Harlow admired his tight ass encased in cargo shorts. He wore a light t-shirt that fit just snug enough to outline the muscles of his back and chest perfectly. She checked her mouth for drool and sighed. Toby was made for temptation—completely delectable—a man of sex, sin, and fun. But he was also fiercely loyal, hardworking, and he loved hard once he let down those walls. Anyone could tell if they looked close enough. It was the way he took pride in the shop, the hours he put into it, and the way he acted when he was around the people he was closest to, like Mel, Carson, Dee, and Rebel. She imagined it was the same with Ash, too.

"Here we are." He turned to face her once he stopped in front of his own ride, but it wasn't the Jeep that caught her attention or the man she'd been fantasizing about just a moment before. It was the badass Harley parked to his right.

"No way." Harlow moved around him and lovingly caressed the satin chrome finishes. "My father had one of these when I was growing up, and I used to love riding with him." She cherished those memories.

"I'll have to take you out on it sometime." Toby smirked as he watched her reaction.

"It's yours?" she asked. "Don't tease me, now."

"Wouldn't dream of it."

"And here I had to go and wear a dress," she pouted. "We could've gone for a ride tonight."

"Gives us another excuse to get together again, now doesn't it?"

"It's a date!" she exclaimed. "I'm really going to look forward to it, too."

"Good to know," he said. "Ready to hit the road?"

"If we must." She sighed, took one last longing look toward the black Fat Boy, and hopped into the waiting Jeep.

Her updo was less than perfect once they arrived at the restaurant, but it was worth it to have the top down and feel the wind course through her hair during the drive. There was something liberating about throwing her hands up, closing her eyes, and enjoying the feel of the elements that surrounded her without a care in the world. It was both relaxing and freeing at once.

Toby got out and quickly made his way to her side to help her out. He searched her face and smirked as he tucked a strand of hair behind her ear. "You're remarkable. You know that?"

"That's me," Harlow replied with more confidence than she felt. Her stomach chose that moment to grumble loudly. "Apparently, I'm also hungry."

"I see that," Toby said. "Shall we?"

She took his arm and followed him across the parking lot.

Mecca's was an oasis of rustic elegance. From the wooden ceiling, to the dimly lit crystal chandeliers above each table. There was light, plush carpeting, a coat room, which they didn't need, and a long bar on the right side of the foyer. To the left stood a very refined-looking hostess.

"Reservation for James, party of two," she overheard Toby say as she admired their surroundings.

"Yes, follow me."

She was met with the warmth of Toby's hand at her lower back again and couldn't help but shiver at the contact as they followed behind the hostess until they reached their table. At that moment, he pulled her chair out for her, and she smiled widely. "Such a gentleman."

"Not often." Toby cleared his throat. "I'm a little rusty." The tinge of pink in his cheeks was endearing.

"Do you come here often? It's a great spot for a date."

And there comes the verbal vomit.

Now it was her turn to blush as she continued to stammer. "Um, not that tonight is a date or anything. It's just…" She gestured around them and left the sentence hanging.

"I get you." Toby placed his hand on top of hers from across the table to stop her from fidgeting. "You're different, and I wanted to take you some place nice. End of story."

"Different how?" she asked. "I'm just a regular girl, taking life one day at a time. Like the rest of you."

"See, that's were your wrong." He sighed and leaned back in his chair. "From the moment we met, I could tell you were different than what I was used to. You're smart and beautiful and one of the strongest women I've ever had the pleasure to meet. I know loss, Harlow. It's not the same as yours exactly, but it still fucks me up. You, on the other hand," he shrugged, "I guess when I see you, I see what hope looks like. You've hit bottom and crawled back to the top. You help people and honor your daughter's memory. I see it, and I admire you for it."

It was her turn to reach out to him. She took his

hand in hers and leaned forward. "That is the nicest thing anyone has ever said to me. I think I might cry."

"Shit, please don't." He rubbed the hand she wasn't holding across his face. "I didn't mean to upset you."

"They'd be happy tears, I promise." She blinked a few times to gain composure. "But I won't. If there is anything I can do for you, if ever you need to talk…"

Toby nodded, but he didn't have a chance to answer. The waiter approached to get their drink orders, and when he left again, the amazingly complicated man across from her changed the subject.

"You know what you want?" He picked up the menu to study it, so she followed suit and did the same.

"The filet mignon looks good, with the rosemary-roasted potatoes and glazed carrots on the side."

He nodded as he closed the menu. "I'm going with the porterhouse, medium, with a side of sweet potato fries."

"Good choice." Harlow took a sip of water. "Were you able to check your schedule? The outline healed well. At least the itching has stopped, but I've been applying lotion liberally."

"Uh, yeah, but I left it at home. You mind coming up for a few when we're done here? You still need to show me those mad drawing skills, remember?"

"Oh, no," she grimaced. "You really want to see

my stick figures that badly?"

"I do." He chuckled, and it was nice to see him at ease again. When she asked how he thought she was different, she hadn't expected such a sweet answer.

Their drinks arrived, their orders were soon placed, and in the meantime, they played a game of twenty questions to get to know one another. It was fun, they kept it light, and she soon learned his favorite color used to be blue, but now it was green, for some reason. Besides Love the Sinner, his favorite band was Shinedown. He was a Minnesota native. He'd known Carson and Mel since childhood. Out of all his family, he was closest to his cousin Ash, and he'd always aspired to be a tattooist.

They ate, they talked, they laughed, and they toasted to new beginnings, memories, and friendship together.

It was a great time.

Chapter Thirteen

Dear Harlow:
Let me start by saying my boyfriend and I have been together for a year now, and we work together but in different departments. Things have been going well enough, but there's this new girl at work who keeps flirting with him and it's pissing me off. What should I do?
~Jealousy Sucks, Minnesota Girl~

*

Dear Minnesota Girl:
Jealousy does suck, but it's a common emotion. My question is: how does your boyfriend react to this flirting? It's hard to give you the right advice when I don't know the whole story. Go with your gut. If he's engaging

91

in an inappropriate manner with this woman, then that's being disrespectful. Kick him to the curb. But if he's innocent in this and doesn't appreciate her advances, then maybe you should both talk to her so she'll knock it off. If that doesn't work out, you may have to report it to human resources.

Good luck,
Harlow

***

TOBY

Harlow sat on Toby's couch, waiting as he grabbed them a drink from the kitchen. Toby also snatched his calendar on the way and soon returned to sit next to her. His heart felt like it stuttered as he saw her face light up when she looked at him. "Here's your beer."

"Thank you," she said as she took a sip before placing the bottle on the wooden coffee table in front of them. She smoothed out her dress where it touched her thighs, and he gulped before clearing his throat. Toby looked away for a minute and came back to his senses. It was too quiet for his liking.

Then talk, dumbass!

"Right, so, about that appointment…" He opened his schedule and flipped through the pages. "I've got an opening Friday, next week. Would you be available?"

"What time?" Harlow asked as she reached for

her purse on the next cushion and rummaged through it to grab her phone. She scrolled through, and he didn't answer her until she seemed ready for it.

"Evening work for you? I've got a six-thirty open. If not, we can do the following Tuesday at three."

"Friday's good." She smiled, typed it into her phone as a reminder, and dumped the cell back into her bag again.

"Next Friday night's all yours, then," he confirmed as he pencilled her in.

"After this tattoo, are you free to take me for that ride, too?" She turned to face him and held her hands together, looking hopeful. It made him laugh. She was so darn cute.

"Got the hots for my Harley, do you?"

"I totally do," she said. "Me and that Fat Boy need to be introduced properly. I should take a picture of me standing beside it and send it to my dad. It would absolutely make his day. Did you know he still has the one he used to take me out on in his garage? He doesn't get to take it out as much as he used to, though."

"Oh, and why is that?" Toby asked.

"Now that they're retired, Mom likes to travel abroad. They're gone half the year."

"Happy wife, happy life," he commented then took a drink.

"About that bike ride…can we?" She brought her hands up and pretended to beg.

"I could swing it. I ride all the time, and believe me, it is not a chore to take a beautiful woman along." He winked, and she blushed. He loved her reactions to such a simple compliment, and it was kind of nice to know he affected her that way. The attraction was certainly mutual, no matter how much he tried to fight it. "As long as you don't mind riding at night. You'll be my last appointment for the day, and the tattoo will take some time to finish, but afterward, I'd be free to take you anywhere."

"Sounds like a good plan." Harlow nodded and stood up. She took her beer with her and walked to the opposite wall. He watched her closely as she admired the artwork, and he could tell she was suddenly nervous. He stood up to follow, and she stiffened when he spoke. "I did that in an art class I took in my early twenties, just for fun." He motioned toward the canvas, which showed an attractive, shapely woman laying down on a chaise with nothing but a blanket covering her lower half. "I don't normally paint. I prefer to draw, but I liked this one, so I put it up."

"I-it's beautiful." she whispered, not looking at him. Then she chugged the rest of her beer.

"Hey, are you okay?" Toby reached out to her, gently took a hold of her arm, and turned her so she faced him again.

"You really want me to draw for you?" she asked. "Your work is so amazing, and I could never be as good."

"Are you nervous because I wanted to see how well you drew a picture?" She had a way of catching him off-guard. "I'd never make you do something you're uncomfortable with; no pressure.

You know that, right?"

She nodded again and took a deep breath. "It's not that, per se. Oh, to hell with it. Hand me a pad of paper and a pencil and tell me what you want me to draw. Don't say I didn't warn you, though."

"You sure?" He had to make certain. Something was going on in that head of hers, and she wasn't sharing whatever that seemed to be.

"I might need another one of those, but yeah, I'm good." Harlow pointed to her empty drink and smiled. "Thanks, Toby."

"I think I can manage that request, too. Just promise to drink this one slower for me, will you?"

It took no longer than a minute or two before they were back where they started, sitting side by side on the couch. He pulled the coffee table closer and placed a sketch pad in front of her with a pencil. He tore a sheet off and placed one in front of him, as well, and positioned their drinks out of the way.

"Let's try a flower. Take your pick."

"You pick. I insist." She shook her head and looked at him like he was crazy for leaving it up to her to decide. Another point on the cuteness scale on her behalf. Toby shook his head and smiled.

"All right. Show me your best sunflower, then." He sat back as she struggled through his request, and it was no joke. Drawing was not her forte. It looked like a sad version of a fuzzy circle with a stick jutting out the bottom.

"You see? It's the suckiest, saddest flower on the planet." She pouted.

Toby's lips twitched, and he fought hard not to laugh because the last thing he wanted was to insult her, so instead, he just brushed it off and decided to help her.

"Okay, let's try this." He ripped her picture from the pad, revealing a fresh page. "Sometimes it helps to break it all down into steps. Follow me. First, draw a big circle and a smaller one in the center." He looked over to make sure she was following his instructions. He was trying to make it as simple as he could, so he was drawing it on his paper as he explained. "Then comes the stem and two leaves on each side of it. Good, now let's draw a thin, elongated, upside-down heart shape that connects to the smaller circle in the middle all the way around, like so." It took her a few tries, but she got the hang of it after a few minutes. He continued. "Add more petals like this to cover up the empty spaces in between and draw slanted lines crisscrossed over each other inside the small circle. Now we erase the outer large circle around, define the stem and leaves by adding a few lines like so, and *voila*! You now have your sunflower complete." He took his drawing, set it beside hers, and smiled. "Proud of you. That's a great-looking flower."

"I actually did it. It's clear, too." She laughed as if shocked. "Yay!" She pumped her hands in the air and her face lit up with excitement.

"Fuckin' adorable." He shook his head again and was pleasantly shocked when she threw her arms around him in a giant hug. This night was looking up, and the more time he spent with her, the more he seemed to enjoy himself. He had almost forgotten what it was like to have someone hug him just because, and it was nice.

Chapter Fourteen

HARLOW

Once she threw her arms around him, Harlow lost the fight. Earlier, she'd been struggling with her attraction for the man, not knowing whether the feelings were reciprocated. But now that she was so close, she thought, what the heck?

Would it be so terrible to just give in for once? To let go, have some fun, and enjoy the long overdue intimacy between a man and a woman?

She'd soon find out.

Toby's arms felt so right round her. He was strong, warm, and felt good pressed against her, breast to chest. He was hard all over compared to her soft curves, and she wanted to explore this spark between them to see where they'd end up.

"I know I've said it before, but thank you." Harlow leaned back slightly to look at him. Her arms moved from around his back and rested around his shoulders. She hadn't wanted to move too far away just yet. She could feel her heart beating inside of her chest as she gauged his reaction to her closeness. Toby licked his lips, and she nearly groaned. "Dinner was sublime. You actually got me to draw a decent enough picture. I'm seriously still shocked that you accomplished that feat." She smiled. "Just goes to show you how talented you really are, but most importantly, I like your company." She leaned forward to press her lips against his. He stiffened momentarily as she kissed him softly, one peck and then two. She nibbled on his bottom lip and sucked on it before letting it go with a pop. Toby moaned and wrapped his arms around her tighter. She trembled as he took over the kiss. The moment she felt his tongue, she opened for him. One hand fisted into her hair, while his other held onto the back of her shirt. Toby tilted his head to deepen the kiss, and before she knew it, she was sitting on his lap and dry humping him. It was amazing. Their accelerated breaths mingled, and for the next few minutes, they were nothing but tongue and teeth—totally absorbed.

Toby pulled back, and she was breathless. Her chest heaved, her nipples pebbled, and she was completely enraptured by him. She was in such a Toby-filled fog, it took her a minute to figure out he'd spoken.

"Harlow?"

"Um, yeah?" She bit her lip, and it made him smile.

"What am I going to do with you?" he asked. She figured he was mostly talking to himself because he didn't wait for her to answer. "As amazing as that kiss was, I'm not sure it was such a good idea."

"Okay." She nodded. "Um…" She licked her lips and wondered what the hell was wrong with her. "It felt good to me."

"Christ, you don't even realize how tempting you are." Toby growled but made no move to push her off his lap. Instead, he placed both hands on her hips and slightly squeezed as if he was having his own internal battle.

Harlow wasn't even sure how to answer him. Tempting? Her? He needed to look in the mirror. If anyone exuded temptation, it was him. She was so out of her element and clearly doing a shit job at trying to seduce him.

"You're right," she replied. "It's probably a bad idea." Her face heated with embarrassment, and Toby surprised her yet again.

"With you, it'd be the best kind of bad. Believe me, baby. Fuck being reasonable, one taste and I'm already hooked." He pulled her forward, so their breath mingled, lips just an inch apart, and whispered, "Not sure I have forever in me anymore, so I can only promise you tonight. You good with that?"

"One day at a time, and no promises," she whispered back as she closed the distance. The kiss was amazing. So magical, it curled her toes, and butterflies took flight inside her belly with excitement. The guy oozed sex appeal as he devoured her mouth. Harlow fiddled with the hem of his shirt and broke the kiss just long enough for her to get the garment off and throw it behind her. Toby soon did the same with her dress. He got rid of her bra too and began to play with her breasts. He rubbed her erect nipples and palmed her boobs in each hand. They were both half-naked, skin against skin, and it was pure bliss to finally feel him up close, in such a personal way. Tonight was their night, and nothing else mattered for once but this moment with him.

Toby's lips trailed down her neck, going lower and lower to taste her everywhere. She squealed with delight as he stood, taking her with him to the very large bed on the other side of the room. She bounced as he threw her on it, and he made quick work of pulling off her underwear, too. He stood back and admired the sight of her, so she decided to reciprocate. His tan chest rippled with overlapping muscle, defined pecs, and abs full of ink. A large, shaded, black and white skull sat right above his heart with a background of orange flames. Two roses sat on each shoulder so big it looked like one big piece. It was beautiful. A pair of lips was tattooed along the sexy V that led to the hard cock she was about to play with, with the words *Only God can judge me* underneath in script. Praying hands with rosary beads was on the other side of it on the left.

"You're beautiful, Toby, and sometime soon, I'd like to trace those tattoos with my tongue, examine them, and maybe figure out their meaning." She smiled, sat up on her knees, and moved closer so she could touch him again.

"Should be my line. Damn, Harlow, you're exquisite—like an angel of sexy innocence. I'm drooling over here because I'm about to eat that pretty pussy, and I already know your taste will be an addiction, then I'm going to want to dirty you up, fuck you until you can't walk, ruin you for any other man."

"Yes, please." Harlow nodded and licked his pierced nipple. "Taste me. Let me taste you. I don't care. I just need…"

Toby growled and pushed her back onto the bed so she was lying flat on her back again. She squirmed and cupped her breasts to tease him. She needed everything he promised and then some. She craved it.

"I know what you need. Fuck me, I know." Toby dropped to his knees. He grabbed her by the ankles and yanked her closer to the edge. When she was into the position he wanted, he threw her legs over his shoulders and feasted. She gasped the minute he licked her from ass to clit. She watched Toby look up in time to see her writhe for him and he watched as she gripped the sheets. She pushed her pussy up into his face to get as close as possible while he licked, flicked, and fucked her with his tongue, and it felt so good, better than she could remember. Her chest heaved with heavy breaths, her body broke out in goosebumps, and her back arched as she screamed out his name in ecstasy. There was a heaven, after all. Hallelujah! Her orgasm came on quickly but lasted so long, she had to beg him to stop so she could take a deep breath. It was bitter sweet bliss.

Toby stood, wiped her juices from his face, and eagerly whipped his pants, boxer briefs, and socks off. He hopped around, and she giggled when he almost lost his footing. He ignored her to grab a strip of condoms from his bedside table and quickly sheathed himself in the latex. God, but he made her breathless just by looking at him. His cock was long, thick, and slightly curved to the right. She licked her lips and slid herself higher on top of the bed so it was easier for him to crawl on top. He growled the moment his dick met her moist pussy, and he rubbed the head against her clit. Harlow shivered and wasn't above begging. She needed him so much. She felt so empty. "Toby, please…"

"Fuck, yes!" he exclaimed.

She felt their spark ignite into an inferno of passion as soon as he entered her.

Chapter Fifteen

TOBY

Holy shit!

He needed a minute or he was about to bust a nut. And there was no fucking way he was going to let that happen so soon. He'd wanted to be in this position from the moment he'd laid eyes on Ms. Hottie, and he wasn't about to ruin it by acting like this was his first time. Christ, she was tight. Perfect underneath him.

"Toby?" Her whisper was nearly his undoing.

"I just need to savor this for a minute," he said then met her halfway in a kiss. He finally began to move, thrusting slowly because it felt too good to rush through it while he made love to her, not only with his dick but with his mouth too. Harlow pulled away and gasped for air. Her hips flexed in tune with his, meeting him thrust for thrust. Her nails trailed down his arms and back up again, leaving slight red marks along the way. Loved knowing that later, whenever he looked in the mirror and saw those little scratches, he'd be treated with this very memory of her. Dark hair spread out against his white sheets, chest heaving, tits bouncing, green eyes on him like he hung the moon. He licked up her neck and nibbled on her lobe. She shivered against him as he breathed her in and whispered sweet nothings in her ear. "You feel so good, Harlow. So tight, warm, and wet on my cock. I want to feel you pulse against me, coming so hard you milk my cock inside of you. Not sure one night is going to be enough with you, and that's all I'm normally made of. I knew you'd be different," he confessed and began to fuck her faster, his own words working him up into a frenzy, and she sighed with satisfaction.

"More, Toby. Harder." She slapped his ass, and it made him chuckle.

"Oh, baby, you asked for it."

He was about to break the fucking headboard. The bed creaked and slammed against the wall, and he didn't care who heard; this woman, his for the taking, was about to scream once again, and it was going to be louder than the last time, if he could help it. He cupped his hands underneath her butt to change positions. Now on his knees with Harlow's lower half elevated, it was like watching his very own porno with him in a starring role. As soon as he was sure Harlow was supported by her legs, he kept one hand squeezing her butt as he fucked her, and his other went up to play with her clit. She was so slick and aroused, she quivered within a minute of his touch and lit up like a firework on the Fourth of July. It was beauty. It was bliss. It was freaking phenomenal, and he could swear he nearly blacked out as her pussy strangled his cock and drained him dry. He collapsed to the side, trying to catch his breath, and he could swear it had never felt like this, not once, or at least, not in a very long-ass time.

One thing was for sure—they'd be doing this again. He was too selfish. It felt too good not to. He just needed to be careful.

By the time he'd come back to his senses, Harlow was cuddled next to him, her head on his chest. Her fingers trailed along the skull over his heart, tracing it. "I know this is the part where I should probably get dressed and go, right?" She lifted her head to look at him, as if waiting for his direction. "It's been a while since I've done this, so I'm not caught up on protocol."

"Do you want to go?" He lifted his brow. He hadn't planned on asking her to leave, but if she wanted to, he wasn't about to stop her.

"Not really." She shrugged. "This is nice."

"What we did was far from nice." His eyes glittered with amusement. "Stay, then."

"Okay." She sat up, and he whistled when he got a good view of her ass. "My turn to play. You just sit back and relax."

Toby stiffened when she picked up his foot and began to massage it. He was in such a sated haze, he hadn't realized he left his scars on display. He normally hid them. The burns he'd sustained from the fire when he lost Carley were worst around his ankles and feet, and now she was touching him—there.

For fuck's sake.

Harlow sensed something, of course. "You don't have to talk about it." She kissed him softly against the puckered skin she held in her hands. "We all have scars, Toby. Our own stories to tell, when we're ready, and you've seen mine." She gulped and gently placed his foot down, massaging higher up his legs now, working her way up his body. He let out a breath, nodded, and tried to relax again. "I just want to make you feel as good as you've made me." She kissed along his legs and stopped herself when she reached the top of his thigh. Harlow gripped the base of his cock, and having a mind of its own, he started to get hard again. She pulled off the condom and threw it in the trash beside his bed. Then he watched her grab a corner of the flat sheet and wipe him clean. He cursed the moment her lips closed around his tip, and his hips jerked at the feel of her tongue swiping the sensitive slit at the top of it before she enclosed her entire mouth down his length until he hit the back of her throat. The moment was epic, and he knew without a doubt, nobody was getting any sleep tonight.

He didn't mind one bit.

Chapter Sixteen

TOBY

"The fuck you laughing at?"

The minute Carson entered the break room, he noticed Rebel sitting at the table with his feet up. He was holding a magazine and chuckling loudly. If his fellow tattooist found something funny, he wanted in on it.

"Shit, man. Toby's girl has some doozies. Check this out."

"Not my girl, Reb," was Toby's instant reply.

"If you say so," Carson said, rolling his eyes. He turned to face Rebel. "You're reading the chick column?"

"Meh," Rebel shrugged. "Since Harlow's been hanging out, I figure I'd see what the fuss was about. Some of it is the standard advice column stuff, some of it is Harlow adding a personal touch to the situation she's replying to. But then you'll read crap like this and we've all been there, but just hearing it, or should I say reading about it, is funny shit." He pointed to a paragraph, and it piqued Toby and Carson's curiosity, so they began to read it over his shoulder.

Dear Harlow:

I know not many men write in, but I have a situation I need help with, and I'm hoping none of my boys will figure out I wrote to you here, no offense. I just don't know who else I can turn to with this. There's this girl I've been seeing for the last two months, and I like her a whole lot. We have fun, she's sweet, and we've got chemistry, if you know what I mean. There is no problem there. Except last week we had a mishap in the sheets that turned embarrassing, and things have been awkward ever since.

Here's the deal, long story short. My girl and I were in the middle of getting busy, and it was good too, until my dumbass roommate barged in on us. To make matters worse, when I went to say what the fu—udge, she farted and not the normal kind. She was mortified, but the coochie bomb was already out there, and I was stunned. In my defense, I don't think anyone is fully prepared when this happens. My roomie laughed, she cried out in misery, and while she hurried to hide under the covers, I was able to recover enough to throw the arse out of my bedroom with a few choice words before slamming the door. I tried

comforting her, holding her, but the moment had passed, and she didn't want to be touched, so I respected her wishes and backed off for the moment. She wanted to go home. To make matters worse, on our way out, my roommate was an ass yet again when he lifted his leg, farted loudly, then told her everybody does it, like it was no big deal. He's lucky I haven't seen him in a couple days.

In the meantime, I call her every day to let her know I'm thinking of her, and we've gotten together once for dinner and a movie, but we haven't been physical since. Is there anything I can do to help her get over the embarrassment?

From,

A Man with a Situation.

"Damn!" Toby said, shaking his head. "Sounds like his roommate needs a lesson in boundaries and a good ass kicking."

"Dude," Carson responded. "My thoughts exactly. He just cock-blocked the guy. What a total douche. It's not like the guy could climb back on and ride that ripple. Sounds like he really likes this chick too. Poor sap."

Toby turned to address Rebel. "What's so funny about this?"

Rebel shrugged. "I was just picturing the scenario, is all. The guy called it a 'coochie bomb,' for fuck's sakes. Guess it's easier to find it funny when it's not happening to you."

"So, what's Harlow say, I wonder?" Carson asked. They both started reading again, assuming Rebel already had.

Dear Situation:

Sounds to me like your roommate needs a lesson in etiquette. Did he realize you were entertaining? I guess it's pointless to ask because the damage has been done. However, I can tell you care about this woman. You did the right thing by respecting her wishes afterward, and I'm sure she appreciates your daily calls just to let her know you're thinking about her. She may need to take things slowly to gain back her confidence, so try to be patient with her. It sounds like you're taking all the right steps.

I can certainly understand why she would be embarrassed, but she's not alone.

Have you tried talking to her about the situation? Communication is key to a healthy relationship. I'm sorry, but I don't have one right answer for you.

Maybe you can try apologizing. What happened isn't your fault. However, she may feel better to hear it. Or maybe you can share an embarrassing experience of your own, so she can feel like you're on even ground.

You mentioned not seeing your roommate

for a few days. I suggest when you do that you mention the predicament he's put you in and set him straight. Let her know he's been handled, and if you can give her reassurance that his lack of boundaries won't happen again, it might help matters as well. I wish you the best of luck in your relationship, and I hope everything works out the way you'd like it to. You sound like a really great guy, and I hope your girl realizes it.

Best wishes,
Harlow

"Smart woman you have there. Don't you think?" Rebel smirked.

"Smart, beautiful, broken, successful, and so much more. You don't know the half of it. I'm just getting to know her, and so far, she's nothing short of remarkable. It's scary." Toby sighed.

"Don't tell anyone I said this, but this chick column is not bad," Carson said, still reading on.

"I heard that." Dee grinned. "Welcome to the dark side." She leaned against the doorframe and crossed her arms. "Hey, Mel, you've got to see this. The guys are reading Harlow Helps."

"Get out!" Mel said as she strolled through the door. "I was wondering where everyone was. We're opening soon, and nobody was out front."

"We've got time, but speaking of the dark side, my darling Dee, are you related to Yoda? Because yodalicious." Carson wiggled his eyebrows up and down, and everyone started laughing.

"Yoda wasn't on the dark side, dumb ass," Mel retorted. "Where do you come up with this shit?"

"It's a gift." Carson shrugged. "And the ladies love it."

"Says you," she replied.

"All right. That's enough sibling banter for one morning. We've got a shop to open." Toby clapped his hands together and watched as everyone filed out.

"Hey, Tob?" Dee stopped at the doorway while everyone went ahead. "I overheard what you said to the guys about Harlow, and I can understand why you'd think it was scary, but life's too short for regrets. It may not be my business, but I'm going to lay it out there anyway. You're a friend, and I care, so sue me." She took a breath. "Carley would have wanted to see you with someone genuine. She would've wanted you to be happy, and you deserve it all, so take the shot if you can and live a little."

"Duly noted," he said. "Now if you don't mind, we have a day to get started, and I'm not in the mood for a heart to heart."

"Right." Dee saluted him, and as she turned around to leave, he called out to her.

"Hey, Dee?"

"Yeah?" She looked over her shoulder at him.

"Thanks. I know you're coming from a good place. I just have to figure out if I'm ready for that advice."

"Well, think about it." She smiled and left.

"One day at a time," he murmured to himself, thinking of Harlow's words when he told her he wasn't sure if he had forever in him anymore. "No promises."

Chapter Seventeen

HARLOW

"So, tell me all about it. I bet it was so good, wasn't it?" Calista bounced on the edge of her seat as she tried prying the details out of Harlow about her night out with Toby. "Your first time out with a man in I can't even remember. Where did he take you?"

"Whoa, calm down." Harlow chuckled. "We went to Mecca's and had a steak. It was delicious. Hey, did you know he lives on top of the shop? I had no idea until the other night."

"No, I didn't, but then again, I never asked." She grabbed her glass of wine and took the last sip. "I need a top up before you continue. Want one?"

"No, I'm good," Harlow said. "But help yourself. You know where the kitchen is."

"Right, keep talking. I can hear you as I pour," her friend called out. They were in Harlow's small apartment having a glass of wine in her living room. It had been three days since she'd spent the night with Toby, and she hadn't heard from him since. In his defense, she hadn't bothered to contact him, either, but she'd wanted to. It was so complicated with all these feelings and confusion. She decided to call Calista so she could talk about everything without her thoughts driving her wild. Plus, she hadn't had the best track record with men, and she needed her best friend's opinion on a few things.

"Well, we went out to dinner, and I fell in love with his bike. He's got this sleek, black Harley I'd love to ride. My dad used to take me out on his when I lived at home, and seeing the motorcycle made me realise how much I missed it, you know? The thrill of the ride, the wind against me, the speed, the freedom."

"I bet that's not the only thing you'd like to ride," Calista teased.

Harlow picked up a decorative couch cushion and threw it at her, narrowly missing the glass she held in her hand.

"Hey, careful."

Harlow smiled. "There is that," she said with a sigh, and it made Calista look at her with wide eyes.

"You didn't. Get out!" Her friend put the drink down and rubbed her hands together in glee. "Oh my God. You did. You hussy, you. I love it!"

"I did. He did. It was incredible, Callie." Harlow clasped her chest and fell back against the couch. "And I'm scared because I'm beginning to have some serious feelings for the guy. I'm not sure he can return them. I mean, he told me he wasn't sure he could give me more than the night we had, and it was like I was possessed with the need to be with him at least once. You know, I just kept thinking, I needed to let go, live in the moment, and have a little fun for once. I always put everyone else before myself, and, well, this time it was different. I went for it."

"It's about time." Calista beamed. "You were well past due to get laid. I was afraid your lady bits might have shrivelled up. A born-again virgin, perhaps. And those cobwebs needed a good poking to clear out or something."

"Oh, shut up." Harlow sat up. "I do not have cobwebs, and nothing shrivelled up, weirdo."

"I know." Calista winked. "I just like teasing you. On a serious note, I'm happy for you." Harlow reached over and held her hand.

"You're a good friend, Callie. Thank you."

"Of course." Calista squeezed her hand. "But let's back up for a minute. What happened after dinner?"

"We went back to his place. He has a really nice loft apartment with these huge industrial windows. Everything is one big open space. It's rustic and modern. Anyway, pretty much right off, we made plans to finish my tattoo. I have an appointment on Friday at six-thirty." Harlow continued, "We're sitting there having a beer and suddenly, I got nervous because I remembered he also said he wanted to see me draw for him. I totally suck. That worry on top of the chemistry I felt brewing between us…I couldn't help it. I got up and admired one of his paintings. I tried to warn him I wasn't any good, and he somehow put me at ease, and we sat back down, side by side, and he taught me to

116

draw a sunflower. It completely surprised me that I actually drew something discernable with his instruction, and I felt elated. It was such a small accomplishment, but there it was. In the heat of the moment, I hugged him. The hug turned into a kiss and the kiss led to—other things."

"Incredible things, as I recall," Calista said.

"They were. It was." Harlow's shoulders dropped, and she looked down at her lap. "I haven't spoken to him since, and it's driving me crazy."

"Wait a minute. You're seeing him on Friday, right? Did you make any other plans?" her friend inquired.

"Friday night, after the tattoo, he's taking me out on his Harley." Harlow looked up and smiled.

"That's good. So why are you going crazy?" Callie smiled back. "He clearly wants to see you again, or he wouldn't have offered you more of his time after the appointment. My guess is, he hasn't called yet because he's crazy busy at the shop. Pick up the phone and call him yourself, if you want to hear his voice. You're a grown, independent woman. You don't need to wait around for a man to make the first move."

"You see? That's why I love you." Harlow nudged her playfully. "I'm going crazy with all kinds of what if's and insecurities because he is so out of my league. He's experienced and I'm—not. And here you are telling me how it is and talking sense."

"I knew I was good for something," Calista laughed. "You lucky girl."

"I'm not sure luck has anything to do with it."

Harlow raised her glass to toast. "Here's to taking chances after so much heartache and hoping it all works out in the end."

"To taking the leap," her friend cheered. "If anyone deserves a happy ending, you do."

"One day at a time, with no promises," Harlow muttered, then took a big sip.

***

It was getting late, Calista had left about an hour earlier, and Harlow sat on the edge of her bed with the phone in her hand.

Here goes nothing.

She eyed Toby's business card beside her and dialed. It rang a few times, and just as she was about to hang up, he answered.

"Hello?"

"Hey, Toby. It's me." She cleared her throat. "Harlow. I didn't wake you up, did I?"

"No. I was just working on a sketch," he replied. "How are you?"

"I'm good. I was just sitting here and thought of you, so I decided to call." She exhaled. "Is this sketch for you or a client?"

"A client," he said. She swore he sounded like he was amused. "It's of a dragon, and it's going to take the length of one arm when I'm finished with it. Just getting the details in there."

"It sounds beautiful," she said.

"Speaking of…what are you up to?" Toby asked.

Harlow giggled. "Did you just imply that I'm beautiful, Mr. James?"

"There is no implying needed. The guys don't call you Hottie Harlow for nothing." The deep timber of his voice gave her shivers, and she laughed as soon as she registered what he had said.

"They do not."

"Oh, but they do." He was amused with this conversation. She could tell. He sounded lighter, happier, even. "Although I may have started it."

"So, you think I'm hot, do you?"

"I think I proved that the other night," he said.

"And then some." She sighed. "Are we okay? The other night was amazing, and you were incredible, but I don't want anything to be awkward between us."

"We're golden, honey. I promise," he assured her. "I'm looking forward to that ride."

"Me too. I can't wait. You know as soon as I walk into Misfit, I'll be all flushed, right? Just fair warning."

"For what?" He chuckled.

"You said the guys call me Hottie Harlow, and now I know it." She giggled. "Walking in was bad enough without knowing. It's like a candy store in there."

"Uh, you lost me there," he said, sounding confused. "We don't sell candy."

She laughed louder. "No, silly. You are the candy. Hot guys as far as the eye can see. Between you, Rebel, and Carson, it's no wonder the girls line up to get ink."

This time, he laughed with her. "It's good to know you think I'm hot, too. The other guys…not so much."

119

"I think I showed you that the other night, didn't I?" She felt cheeky and went with it.

"Fuck me. Did you ever," he recalled. "I may need a repeat performance if you're up for it."

"So, you're not a one and done then? Good to know," she said. "I'd like that."

"I normally am, but with you, I can't seem to get enough," he admitted, and she wondered if it cost him to do so.

"I appreciate your honesty. You're a good man, Toby James. One with many talents."

"Thanks," he replied. "I try."

"You're welcome." Harlow yawned. "Sorry about that. I guess I'm a little tired. Calista came over tonight, and I had a couple glasses of wine."

"Sounds like a good time," Toby said. "I've got to finish the dragon, and you need sleep. We'll talk soon, yeah?"

"You have my number, and I obviously have yours, so yeah, we'll talk soon. Night, Toby."

"Sweet dreams, Hottie Harlow."

Chapter Eighteen

Dear Harlow:
My boyfriend only cares about getting himself off in bed. I love him, but I have needs too. How should I handle this?
~**Unfulfilled in Minnesota**~

*

Dear Unfulfilled:
Be blunt, and if he can't give you what you need, dump him.
Good luck,
Harlow

***

HARLOW

Harlow sighed in relief as she walked into the air

conditioned lobby of Misfit Tattoo. It was Friday, *the* Friday, when she was going to finish her tattoo then go out with Toby. She had butterflies in her stomach at the thought of the finished product on her skin. It meant so much to her: a permanent, beautiful mark that represented life and death intertwined, but it also represented her daughter, in a way. Her precious little girl's memory, that was. It also hid a few of the many scars she struggled with. Then there was Toby—a conundrum of a man she couldn't seem to resist with his sexy good looks, big heart, dedication, and loyalty. But she was also drawn to his darker side. She could recognize the internal struggle inside his gaze, as if he understood her sense of loss and grief. A kindred spirit with whom she also had a deep connection. It might have been her need to help people, including herself, that made that draw more enticing because everyone has those demons inside somewhere. He was just another fellow broken soul who she happened to be falling for fast and hard. Some of the excitement she endured by being there today was also for the man himself.

They'd been busy with work but had talked several times over the week since she'd made the first move by calling him. She looked around at the few people seated in the lobby looking through books, cleared her throat, and pasted a big smile on her face as she approached Rebel and Dee, who looked quite cozy together behind the counter. "Hey, guys. I'm sorry to interrupt."

Rebel winked, and the beautiful receptionist blushed. "Nice to see you, Harlow. I'll just let Toby know you're here." He walked backward, addressing Dee. "We'll talk more later. You can count on it."

"Thanks, Rebel. It's nice to see you again, too." Harlow waved, then arched a brow at her colorful friend with curiosity. "So, you and Rebel, huh?"

"When there's something to tell, I'll let you know." Her friend held up a hand and fanned her face as if to imply there definitely would be a story to tell later.

"You go, girl!" Harlow giggled as Dee gave her a high five. "Hey, what's Mel up to? I was hoping to say hello."

Dee pointed behind her. "She's in back doing a Prince Albert."

"A Prince who?"

"You're hilarious." Dee chuckled. "It's a piercing on a guy's…" When she pointed to her crotch, it was Harlow's turn to blush.

"Well, okay, then." She cleared her throat. "That sounds painful."

They both turned to the sound of Carson's voice coming from the hallway in the back. "Well, well, well. If it isn't two of my favorite women." He winked and strode toward Harlow until he stood in front of her. He grabbed her hand and continued. "Excuse me. Is your name Earl Grey? Because you look like a hot-tea!"

She was speechless. Literally, she had no idea how to respond to that. Where did he come up with this stuff? Instead, she went with her gut and laughed like usual.

"I can't believe you get laid with those lame-ass

come-ons." Dee shook her head. "Must be your pretty face." She patted his cheek.

"My pretty face and hot bod. Not to mention my many talents. I'm also a sucker for a pretty smile, and those lines work every time." He flexed his arms and blew them both a kiss before he called out to his next client. "Max, my man. You're up, dude."

They both watched him walk back with his canvas in tow, and Harlow sighed. "I'm seriously going to look forward to the day he meets his match. At least, I hope I'm still around to witness it. Underneath that playboy exterior is a great guy, and she'll be one lucky woman."

"Agreed," Dee replied. "Since we're on the subject of good men…yours is coming as we speak. Oh, and if all works out as we're all hoping, you'll be around a while."

"I hope so," she whispered for Dee's ears only.

"What an amazing sight to behold." Toby pulled her behind the counter and into his arms. "Hey, gorgeous. It feels like it's been too long."

"We just spoke yesterday. Miss me already?" She stepped back and smiled.

"You know it," Toby said. "You're my last appointment of the day, so let's get this show on the road. Shall we?" He gestured for her to follow him down the hallway. "We'll finish your artwork and I'll be able to have you all to myself. I've been looking forward to it all week."

"You did miss me." Harlow was elated at the thought. "The feeling is mutual."

"Good to know, baby." The moment they crossed the threshold of his station, he slammed the door to give them privacy and was on her in an instant. Her back was pressed against the door, and the heat of Toby's body surrounded her. His mouth immediately sought hers, and it was heaven on earth. They were both breathless when he pulled away reluctantly. "We'll have to continue that a little bit later because if I don't stop now, there'll be no turning back."

"Something else to look forward to." Harlow smirked and took off her shirt. "You ready for me?" She hopped up on the tattoo table, lay on her side, and got comfortable.

"More than you know," Toby replied. She squealed when he smacked her on the ass as he walked by. It only took a couple minutes for him to set up, and the familiar buzz of the tattoo gun filled the room. "Whatever you're doing, keep it up. The tatt looks like it healed up really well," he said.

"I washed it every day and liberally moisturized." She shrugged. "I can't wait to see the finished product."

"I bet. No regrets?"

Harlow shook her head. "Zero. I guess my initial problem was fear of the unknown—finding someone I trusted enough to get it right and allowing myself to take the leap. Thanks to Calista, Melody, and you, here I am. You came along, listened to the idea I had, and made it better with your crazy, incredible talent. Now, here we are, finishing it, and it's truly incredible. I can't thank you enough."

"No thanks are needed. Trust me when I tell you, the pleasure has been all mine. It makes it that much better when it means something to the person you're giving your art to." They were silent for a minute before Toby continued with a question. "Have you known Calista a long time?"

"We met just before Lily's first birthday, actually." Harlow smiled as she recalled the memory. "She was my neighbor, and she turned out to be a really great friend, as you can tell. My first here in this city. Before her, I mostly kept to myself. I only lived here a couple of months, and I was settling into a new job at St. Paul's in their Family Services Department."

"Where was Lily while you were working?" Toby asked.

"She was with the Coles. They're a friend of the family, of my mom's, actually, and they were happy to help out whenever they could. They adored the both of us."

"That's good. Do you still keep in touch?" he asked.

"Unfortunately, no," she admitted, ashamed to say so. They were good people. "After Lily passed away, it took a long time for me to recover, both physically and emotionally. Hell, I think I'll always be a little broken. Let's face it, losing a child is just something one doesn't ever get over. It's too tragic." She shook her head and took a moment to gather her thoughts. "I was a shell of the person I used to be, and I kept to myself. Sometimes, I thought it was easier to just push people away. The less people you had to care about, the less it would hurt if something were to happen again. I couldn't cope. Know what I mean?"

"I know exactly how that feels," he said but didn't elaborate.

"I somehow knew you would." She sighed. "But Calista was a force to be reckoned with. No matter how much I pushed, she pushed back. It didn't feel like it at the time, but it was kind of a godsend, and she was the rock I needed to lean on until I pulled myself together. The fact is, we need people, especially through the tough times. It's human nature, even if it's just to talk out the issues we hold inside. It took a while for me to figure that one out, by the way."

Toby snorted. "Did it, now? Don't they teach you that when you study psychology?"

"In theory, I guess. But it's a different ballgame to practice what you preach. Think of it this way. Would the person you lost want you to dwell on the grief and live miserable and alone for the rest of your life? Or would they love you enough to want to see you move on and succeed? In order to do that, you need to let people in, talk about it, and go through all the steps you need to grieve so you can get better for yourself and become a stronger person. Loving someone is a blessing, and although I'd give anything to have my daughter back, that's just not my reality anymore. Though I am grateful for the time we had and that I was once blessed to be her mother, even if it was only for a short time."

"Remarkable," Toby said. She drew in a deep breath while he went over a particularly sensitive spot on her skin. "You're a strong person, Harlow Ross. Don't ever let anyone tell you otherwise. It's one of your many qualities, which I admire."

"Uh, thanks." She winced as he began working across her ribs.

"Can I ask what happened with Lily's father? You've never really mentioned him." Toby paused to dip the gun in ink and wiped the spot he was working on with a paper towel before his needle met her skin again.

"There's not much to tell." She cursed. "Shit, that hurts."

"Sorry," he said. "Do you need a break?"

"Maybe just a minute." She sighed when he pulled away. "Lily's father was someone I met in my last year of University. We were together only a few months when I found out I was pregnant, and it didn't go so well when I told him the news. His name was Scott, and he was a pre-med student looking forward to starting a residency at Stanford Hospital. I thought he was incredibly smart and good looking, and we were both young and having fun, until we weren't." She shrugged while staring at the wall in front of her. "I once thought we had the same goals. Anyway, I found out I was pregnant a few months into the relationship, and he freaked out. He accused me of entrapment, made it seem like I had done it on purpose because I wanted to nab a doctor to secure my future, which was preposterous. I was working toward my degree in psychology. I didn't need him or anyone else to secure anything. I was doing fine on my own. We got into this huge argument and broke up. I was devastated, but I was determined to prove him wrong. He avoided me for the rest of my time at school, and I endured the gossip and pitying looks the whole time. By the time I was in my third trimester, I had graduated with honors. So, there you go. Suck it, Scott!" She wiped a tear from her eye and laughed humorlessly. "Then he found out when our little girl died, he must have heard about it on the news or something, and I swear, it was the first time since my last year in university I heard his voice again, but his apology came too little too late. He was never in her life. He didn't want to be. But despite that, I invited him to the funeral to say goodbye, if he wanted to, and the asshole didn't even bother to show up. Can you believe that? I mean, why call me to begin with? I was going through enough at that point. That was the first and last time I heard from him in years, and I hope to God it'll be the last. He's evil and cruel, and I hope karma bites him in the butt."

"If I ever meet him, I guarantee I'll kick his ass for you." Toby stood above her and pressed on her shoulder so she could move from her side to her back and he kissed her forehead. "Fuckin' incredible, I tell you."

"What is?" she whispered.

"You," was his simple reply. "Now, are you ready to get started again?" He moved to sit back on his stool.

"Let's do this." Harlow nodded and moved back onto her side. She lifted her arm and settled her hands together so she could place them under her cheek. "Um, Toby?"

"Yeah?"

"I'd be happy to return the favor someday and listen when you're ready to share your story too."

There was no telling when, or if, that would happen, but there was always hope.

"Maybe someday." His gloved hand lightly squeezed her hip as if acknowledging the offer, and she let it go for now.

One day, she'd find out about his ugly, just as she shared hers with him, and she hoped it would help him heal. Toby was a good man who deserved happiness in the end.

They both did.

Chapter Nineteen

TOBY

He admired her as she stood in front of the floor-length mirror at his station. He'd just finished the shading and coloring of her tattoo, and it was fuckin' beautiful, if he did say so himself. One of his best pieces to date. "As before, the redness should disappear by tomorrow. It'll be sensitive for a few days. Be sure to clean it with soap and water regularly and moisturize. It'll help if it starts to itch." He swallowed. "But you know all that. Would you mind if I take a picture before we wrap it up? With permission, I'd be honored to add it to my portfolio."

When she turned around, he saw tears in her eyes, and it made him want to take her in his arms and protect her from everything and everyone. This woman was amazing and strong. She did things to him and made him feel things he hadn't felt in so long. It felt like ages, another lifetime ago, since his heart had been thawed out and started beating again.

She made him feel again, made him want to become a better person and to take a chance. Would Carley have liked her?

Shit, probably. Who knew for sure?

He rubbed a hand across his face and held back a curse. What he needed was to slow this shit down, but that was easier said than done when he was around her. Since recovering from the burns and trauma—since Carley was taken, as a matter of fact—his coping method involved a revolving door of women and booze to deal with the nightmares and lack of sleep. The shitty depression and anger needed an outlet, and when he wasn't fucking or getting buzzed to dull the pain, he was getting the new shop running and working his ass off. It was exhausting.

After a while, she finally responded. "The honor would be mine. Wow, I knew how beautiful it was going to be. It's just…now that it's done…I don't know." She shrugged. "It's like another chapter of my life has ended and a new one is beginning. Lily would have thought this was so pretty. You would have loved her. I know I mentioned this before, but she always loved to make me drawings for our refrigerator of flowers and anything else that gained her attention."

"I'm sure I would have." He gulped back the heavy feeling in the pit of his stomach, thinking of her little girl, and nodded. There was a time in his life he couldn't wait to have children, and he wondered if he'd ever get there again. At thirty-three, he wasn't getting any younger.

The tattoo went from just under her armpit down

to her hip, taking up her whole side. He could see the scars she covered up, but that was only because he'd known where they'd been. Anyone else probably wouldn't notice them, though. The skull was a large black and white piece which was shaded well, so it looked realistic. The vine of flowers went through the skull, creating a halo at the top, making it look angelic and feminine. Then the vines tapered down her side into a bouquet that spread out and down to her hip bone. Life and death. Perfection on the outside to hide the imperfections she struggled with inside. But who could blame her?

He vowed right then and there that when the time was right, he'd share his story with her, and soon. It was only fair for her to know what she was getting herself into if things went any further between them. He already knew she was different from the rest, and he was broken and totally fucked up. The least he could do was warn her about it before either of them got in too deep.

He didn't love her yet, but he knew without a doubt that he could, and that was some scary shit. He liked her a lot, though, and that wasn't going to change. She was good people right down to her core, inside and out. Beautiful, smart, caring, strong, sweet, and sexy. So sexy.

Harlow was a woman who deserved it all, but did he deserve a woman like her? That was another question altogether. She was the light to his dark.

"Hey, are you okay?"

Her whispered words brought him out of those deep thoughts, and he sighed as he went to grab his phone to take that picture. "Yeah, I guess I sort of zoned out for a minute. Nothing to worry about." He winked, and her smile put him at ease.

"These'll look good." He showed her the two pictures he'd taken on his phone. "This tattoo is one to be proud of."

"It really is," she said. He could see the pride written all over her face. She was really good for his ego.

"Damn right it is." He smirked. "Just give me a sec to cover it up for a bit. You can take it off in an hour or two to air it out." He applied the antibacterial ointment. Once he was sure the area was sterilized, he then placed a plastic wrap on top and taped it to keep any germs or bacteria away from the wound. "On the other hand, forget the hour or two. I'd recommend keeping the wrap on until the morning to be safe, due to the size of it and where the tattoo is located."

"Then morning it is." She rubbed her hands together. "Now about that ride…"

"I didn't forget." Toby chuckled and gave her a kiss on the lips. "But first, you'll need to get dressed. Don't you think?" Her shirt hung from his index finger as he held it up for her, and she snatched it away.

"I think you might be right, silly man." She winked. "It's hot as hades out there, but I also brought a light jacket. A girl can never be too prepared while on a motorcycle. I was taught well."

"I can see that," he said, unable to help himself as his gaze ran from the bottom of her running shoes up to her long legs encased in tight jeans. He continued his perusal up to her shapely hips, flat stomach, great breasts, and didn't stop until he was looking into those gorgeous green eyes, which he had decided were his new favorite color. Her shirt was on now, but he could still tell she was just as affected as he was with their mutual attraction, thanks to her hardened nipples pointing right in his direction. He licked his lips, and his mouth watered. He was a man, after all. "After you." He opened his door and gestured for her to go ahead of him. The entire gang, minus Carson, was out front. He was still with his client and due to close the shop tonight, thanks to his plans with Harlow. Plans he was very much looking forward to.

"There's our girl." Mel smiled and hugged Harlow lightly. "Let me see."

Dee moved closer to have a look too, but Toby moved in faster. "Sorry, me and your girl have a date with my Harley. Maybe next time." Harlow chuckled and looked back with a wave.

"Later, ladies. I'll give you a call. We'll go out for drinks soon. The four of us. I promise."

By the time they made it outside, the sun had already set, and it was getting dark out. There was a light breeze in the air that helped lower the humidity from earlier.

"What's the rush?" The sound of happiness in her voice tugged at his heart and filled him with warmth. A gift only she seemed to give him. He slowed his pace and turned to face her.

He tucked a piece of hair behind her ear and shrugged. "Figured if we didn't get out when we did, those two would have kept us there for a while. Trust me. They know how to talk, and now that my work is done, I was kind of looking forward to having you all to myself." He caressed the side of her face and leaned down for another kiss. The taste of her was becoming his addiction. He sucked on her bottom lip and whispered, "Okay?"

He pulled back just enough to gauge her reaction and knew it was the right move when she pulled him down to devour his mouth.

Chapter Twenty

Dear Harlow:

Is there a time limit to the grieving process?

I lost my husband eight months ago to cancer, and my friends are already encouraging me to move on. It's too soon. I honestly don't know if I'll ever be ready to meet someone else. Help!

~Weeping Widow, Minnesota~

*

Dear Weeping:

First, I'd like to say I'm so sorry for your loss. I know the grieving process well, and I can tell you from experience that there is no time limit on it. I can certainly understand how after only a few months you feel like you aren't ready to be romantically involved again.

Take it one day at a time. You never know what the future will hold. You may feel differently down the road. In the meantime, take care of you. Talk to someone about how you're feeling regularly.

Try not to worry so much about everyone else's expectations.

Big hugs,
Harlow

***

HARLOW

There was nothing more intoxicating and alluring than being on an open road with the wind on her face and flowing through her hair. Or at least the part of her hair that wasn't confined inside a helmet. To hear the roar of a good engine, to feel the vibration between her legs, and to enjoy the openness that surrounded her as she got to view the remarkable sights while they drove by. It made her feel grateful to experience it again. Harlow had never been on a motorcycle ride in Minneapolis before. It was her first time on a bike since she'd left Fresno all those years ago. It didn't hurt that she was also able to enjoy it while her arms were wrapped tightly around the rippling muscles of a gorgeous man, either.

Toby took her along The Grand Rounds, which encompassed some lakes, creeks, woods, and riverbanks. It was so resplendent with natural features. It also had canals, lagoons, parks, and so much more. It was dark, but what she could make out through the street lighting was breathtaking. She'd have to come back again one day to get a closer look.

About an hour later, Toby steered them back in the direction of the shop. The time flew by so fast, she didn't want it to end. Thankfully, neither did he.

"Was it as good as you remembered?" Toby smirked while he helped her get the helmet off. Her legs were a little shaky as she got off the back, but she managed the feat on her own.

"Oh, yeah." She chuckled. "When can we go again?"

He laughed with her. "Anytime you want. Would you like to come up for a drink?" He gestured toward his loft upstairs and placed an arm around her shoulders.

Harlow nodded. "What a rush."

When they stepped inside Toby's apartment, she twirled herself around with enthusiasm and sat on his couch, as if in a daze. Toby shook his head with amusement and tossed his keys on the kitchen counter. He opened the refrigerator.

"Glad you think so. Not every woman can appreciate the experience. It's refreshing to see that you do."

"Calista once told me she thinks they're death traps." Harlow shrugged. "To each their own, I guess. I obviously got my love for motorcycles from my dad. We both did growing up."

"We, as in…" Toby looked up at her.

"My sister and I." Harlow smiled. "We're eleven months apart. She's younger. I don't see or hear from her very much. Harper is an English teacher overseas."

"I see. Is it just the two of you?" he asked.

"It is," she replied. "How about you? Are there any James siblings out there?"

"No, just me," he said. Toby stood up with his hands full of food and kicked the refrigerator closed. "I didn't get a chance to eat much earlier. Are you hungry? I've got some leftover pasta and a salad."

"Maybe a little." She held up her forefinger and thumb to show him just how much. "Need any help?" She hopped up and walked to the kitchen before he could answer. He passed her the container with the salad.

"Bowls are in that cupboard." He pointed to her left, and she helped herself while he nuked their pasta. "We've got milk, water, coffee, tea, or soda to go with tonight's late dinner. What'll it be?"

"Water, please." She smiled as he tossed her two bottles, and she placed them beside the salad bowls on his small kitchen table. A few minutes later, Toby joined her at the table with two plates, one in each hand. He placed one in front of her and went to get them some utensils.

"Dig in."

There was a comfortable silence between the two of them while they ate. When they were done, she insisted on helping him out with the dishes.

"How's the side?" Toby asked as he leaned against the kitchen counter. "Are you itching to take off the wrapping yet?"

"My very talented tattooist suggested I keep it on until morning," Harlow replied. "It's a little sensitive, but I'll survive."

"May I?" Toby gestured to the side of her shirt as if to ask permission to lift it up. He wanted to have another look.

Instead of answering, she lifted it up herself and looked down at her new art. "I'm in love with it, I swear." She smiled as she looked at him, and he took a step closer. "My vision is now a reality. How can I not be?"

"You're so fucking good to me." He smirked and gave the tattoo a gentle touch above the clear wrapping. "At least the redness is gone. And it doesn't look like you bled too much. Should heal nicely for you."

"I have no doubt," she said. "You know it goes both ways, right?"

"What does?" When he looked up, she let her shirt fall back into place, and she closed the distance between them. Her hands rested on his pecs, and Toby automatically put his arms around her.

She licked her lips and then explained.

"You're good to me too, and *for* me actually. The first time I saw you, I was instantly intrigued. Here was this very attractive, confident man sporting sexy tattoos, who got me to open up by explaining the tattoo I needed and why I wanted it." Harlow blushed and rested her head against his beating heart. "Then I was in awe with you when you took my idea and made it so beautiful. I mean, I'd imagined it, but what you did seemed to be so much better. I know it doesn't really make sense when I try to explain it, but that's how I felt. I've been alone for such a long time, especially in the romantic sense, and now here I am with you, and I feel so alive. I like you, Toby, and I sense the feeling is mutual. I also know you have your own scars to deal with, whatever they may be, and I'm here for you when you're ready." She took a deep breath, almost dreading the answer to her next question. "Am I scaring you yet?"

"Yes and no." Toby sighed and pressed a kiss to her forehead. "No because I like you, too. And yes because I like you much more than I probably should in such a short time. You're special, Harlow, but I haven't told you my story, and I don't know if I can completely get past it to move on." He stepped back and placed a finger under her chin. He gazed into her eyes and continued. "You deserve everything, and I really want to give that to you, though."

"You and me both," she whispered. "Would you please kiss me already?"

She'd been anticipating this kiss since their last one a few hours ago. She couldn't get enough. His touch and taste had been all she could think about all week. Enough talking. She was ready to put her words into actions. The kiss started out sweet. Toby placed kisses all over her face, starting with her forehead again, then her eyelids, on her nose and finally to her lips. He nibbled on her mouth, took his time, and she savored every second of it. But the moment she opened for him, his tongue finally sought entry, and it soon turned hungry and rough.

142

Toby picked her up, and she gladly wrapped her legs around his waist. He carried her to the other side of the apartment and gently laid her on his bed. Their hands began to explore each other, and she became breathless.

"We've got to be careful of your side. Are you good?" Toby asked. His deep timbre sounded rough with need, and her heart beat a little faster.

"I'll be fine." Harlow bucked her hips up and rolled them both over so that she was on top now. "But how about we let me be in control this time? Just in case." She winked and pulled her shirt above her head to toss into the corner. Her bra soon followed.

"Fuck me. You're hot," Toby replied. "Still too many clothes on."

Harlow agreed and moved over to get rid of the remaining barriers, while Toby did the same for himself. Once they were both completely naked, Toby lay back on the bed and patiently waited for her to join him. He was so tall and built, masculine and sexy, her mouth watered. His hard cock rested against his tattooed stomach, and she licked her lips. She sat beside him and gripped the base of his dick, stroking him from root to tip with her hand. Her other hand fondled his balls, and he thrust his hips up, wanting more. "You're so sexy."

"Took the words right out of my mouth." He panted, "Need you, Harlow. Need more."

"God, yes," she hissed. She wanted the same thing. Harlow leaned over him to replace her hand with her mouth on his shaft. Her ass was in the air for his viewing pleasure. He gripped her hips and pulled her closer to him. Her legs spread, and he maneuvered her so that she was on top, ass to face. She shivered and cried out when Toby latched on to taste her dripping pussy. The more turned on she became, the harder she worked him. Her tongue circled the head of his cock. She licked down the side of it and back up again to taste every inch before she enveloped the entirety of his length inside her mouth to suck. Back and forth, her head bobbed, up and down. He hit the back of her throat, and her gag reflex kicked in. She released him from her mouth like a big old lollypop and stroked him harder with her hand. Toby was magic with pussy, a master at making her come apart. She was so close. She rode his face, knowing she was about to explode. Her breath hitched, her nipples pebbled, and Harlow panted. "Holy shit."

She could tell he was loving her responsiveness when he began to fuck her hand as she jacked him off. "So good, baby. I love that mouth." Her body began to tremble, and she was weak in the knees. "Oh God, Toby!" She couldn't hold back any longer and went off like a rocket into oblivion. It was sweet, sweet bliss. Harlow lay boneless on top of him while he lapped her juices and kissed her thighs. When she was done riding that wave of ecstasy, Toby squeezed her ass and slapped it.

"No more mouth. Give me that pussy."

"Kay." She pushed some hair out of her face and moved so he could grab a condom from his night table beside the bed. He quickly put it on, and she eagerly climbed on top again. He positioned his cock to align with her wet cunt, and she slowly sank inch by inch until he was seated to the root. They both moaned in unison.

She paced herself slowly because it felt way too good to rush. There'd be time for that later. Her hands rested on his chest for leverage while she moved over him. Toby matched her rhythm. He played with her breasts, and she leaned forward to kiss him, couldn't get close enough. Harlow could taste herself on his lips, and it excited her more. They explored each other, were getting to know each other, and she was falling so fast, she needed to catch her breath. She broke the kiss with a gasp and cried out again when Toby's mouth latched onto her boob. Her pace quickened and pussy pulsed. She wanted to make him feel as good as he made her feel and gave it her all. Sweat cascaded down her back, and Toby grabbed onto her ass cheeks to help guide her into a faster pace.

"Feel so good, Harlow." He hissed, "Tight—warm—wet. So close."

Harlow nodded and sucked on her index finger while she bounced. She trailed the digit down her body to her clit and started to rub it. "Me too, baby."

Toby's gaze zeroed in on her ministrations. She knew exactly how to play her body like it was a finely tuned instrument. It wouldn't take her long to erupt again. She was too worked up. "Come, Toby. Fill me up."

"Fuck, yeah!" he hollered, and his cock twitched. Toby held himself still and sighed her name when he finally let go, and that's all it took for her to pulse again with her own release while he filled the condom inside of her.

Chapter Twenty-One

TOBY

She was abso-fuckin-lutely glowing, and his chest swelled with pride. They were breathless and well spent after this first round of making love. If all went according to plan, he could go for another round or ten before exhaustion hit them. But first, they needed to talk. He at least owed her that much. She'd confided in him several times, and he'd given her nothing about himself in return. At least, not the fucked up or important parts. The stuff she needed to know going forward. It was time to man up and spill if he wanted a shot with her, and he needed to do it fast before he changed his mind. This shit wasn't going to be easy.

Toby took a deep breath and exhaled. "I think I'm addicted already."

"What?" Harlow giggled and lifted her face off his chest to look at him.

"To this, us, and the sex is..." Toby grinned when Harlow finished his thought for him.

"Incredible, epic, the best?"

"No doubt." He chuckled and rubbed a hand down his face. They had some serious chemistry; there was no denying it. "I'm going to get cleaned up, then I'd like to talk to you about something."

"Is everything okay?" Harlow sat up and looked adorably confused in all her naked glory. He wished he could have taken a picture right then to capture the memory in case things got too heavy for either of them to handle. This was it, or it would be in a minute or two, but first, he needed to handle the condom.

"Yeah, I just figured it was time to talk about me, my baggage, whatever you want to call it. You've already given me you. It's only fair I do the same," he said. Toby got out of bed and turned away from her to discard the condom. He threw it in the trash and sat back down on the edge of the bed, dreading what came next.

Harlow traced the broken angel wings he'd had tattooed on his back after Carley died and whispered, "If you're sure you're ready, then I'm here for you." She massaged his shoulders, and her touch and encouraging words soothed him enough to go on.

"I don't think I'll ever be ready, truthfully. Talking about this is hard, but I care about you, so I will." Toby leaned forward and rested his head between his hands. "You're special to me, Harlow, and I feel like you understand where I'm coming from."

Harlow kissed him between his shoulder blades and hugged him from behind. "Somehow, I think I

148

might."

"Right," he agreed. "Mel ever tell you how I lost Blank Canvas? My old place. If not, you're about to find out. It's a big part of this shit show I'm stuck with." He didn't bother to wait for an answer. "But first I get to tell you about the best part. Her name was Carley, and she was my fiancé for about five minutes. We were together for a few years, and she was everything to me. She was short and cute as a button. Fierce, loyal, and tough through and through. She'd come into the shop, a tattoo virgin, just like you. Only she wanted to start out small. Got herself this little blue butterfly on her left shoulder. From there, she was hooked into getting a full sleeve and eventually got into piercings, by Mel's influence." Toby exhaled. "We had this magnetism, and she was so easy to be around. You kind of remind me of her a bit in that sense. It was just before Christmas, and she was coming in to get her nipples pierced on the night I proposed. I talked everyone into leaving early so it'd be just the two of us. I had my office all set up with candles and flowers, crap to make it romantic for her. I gave her the nip jewellery, and we headed to the back. Later on, we fell asleep on the couch I had back there with her curled around me. Not sure how long we'd been out, but by the time I woke up, I was drenched in sweat. I had a hard time catching my breath, and I was weak. It was surreal. My eyes opened and closed a few times before I caught my bearings. The place was burning, smoke was everywhere, and I could hardly see. I called out to Carley, but she wasn't responding. When I tried getting up, she

149

rolled to the floor. I couldn't focus, and I knew I had to get us out." Toby finally managed to look behind him to gauge Harlow's reaction and tried to breathe past the tears that threatened to fall. "Managed to drag us out of the burning office but blacked out before I could get us outside. Carley died. The burns on my calves and feet are my reminder."

"Mr. Idiosyncratic?" Harlow whispered in shock. It all made so much sense now. She sprang off the bed and knelt in front of him. "Oh, Toby, I am so sorry."

Toby let out a grunt when Harlow flew into his arms. He had no words. What was somebody supposed to say to that? *You're not the only one.* He hated being broken.

Instead, he just held onto her tightly, and it felt good for the moment. *She* felt good. His heart physically ached at the memory, and he rubbed his chest when she leaned back a couple of inches. What he wasn't expecting was for her to kiss him there. She literally moved his hand out of the way and placed her lips right above his heart.

So sweet. Shit.

Harlow never failed to astound him. He held her hands with both of his. "This is why I'm not sure I can commit to anything long term. I can't make you promises, Harlow, and you deserve them. Losing Carley nearly destroyed me, and the hurt won't fucking go away."

"It's not easy, Toby. I understand. What you went through was heartbreakingly traumatic. It's not something someone can just get over, just like that." She withdrew her hand from one of his and snapped her fingers. "Carley sounds like an amazing woman, and no one should expect you not to feel the way you do. I don't think I'll ever get over the loss of my daughter. What I do know is that I like you a lot. I enjoy spending time with you, and I feel this connection between us. We're two people who, unfortunately, were dealt a shitty hand. Life is hard, but it's also what you make of it. I'm willing to take a chance if you are. Day by day, one date at a time."

"I can handle that." He gave her a sad smile and quickly kissed her on the lips.

"Talking about it helps. I had to see someone for a while after I recovered from my injuries. I don't go as often anymore, but I do if I feel like I need to. Have you ever thought about seeing someone for that?" Harlow asked.

"You mean a shrink?"

"Yeah, it gets easier with time, and it helps with the healing process. I can give you a recommendation if you're interested. No pressure, though." She held a hand to her chest and looked adorable doing it. His mouth twitched to hide a smile, and suddenly, his heart didn't feel so heavy.

She did that for him.

"Not sure I'd like that so much." He shrugged. "But I'll give it some thought."

"Fair enough." Harlow lifted from her knees and hugged him again. Her lush breasts rubbed against his chest, and it stirred his cock back to life. She was incredible, and he wanted her again.

"You're beautiful, baby. Inside and out." Toby

caressed the side of her face and kissed her with everything he had. This time he was going to show how much he appreciated her by going slow with his insatiable need.

Chapter Twenty-Two

Dear Harlow:

I must have the worst luck ever. Three weeks ago, I went out with some friends and met someone. We had a good time, but it was a onetime thing, and I never expected to see him again. Then last week, I go into work to meet my new boss, and it's him. My one-night guy. Talk about awkward.

To make matters worse, just as I'm about to shake his hand, I trip over a chair, land on all fours, and split my pants open. I was mortified, while he seemed to be amused. I've been doing my best to avoid him ever since, but I know I'll have to face him eventually. Any advice?

~Unlucky and Clumsy in Minneapolis~

*

Dear Unlucky:

It sounds like you have the same type of luck I do. I can choke on air and trip over my own two feet at times. It happens to the best of us, but we're all adults here, and as such, we should be able to get past our embarrassing moments. I say go in there and confront it head-on. Act confident, like it never happened, and if he brings it up, laugh it off and move on. Life is too short to dwell on the little things we can't change.

Best wishes,
Harlow

***

HARLOW

"Here are some of my favorite girls." Fanny clasped her hands together and pulled out a chair. "Hey, Harold. I'm on break."

"What?" Fanny's husband hollered from behind the bar.

"I'm taking ten minutes to myself. Hold down the fort, will ya?" she replied and turned to face everyone at the table. "Damn, I love that man, but we're getting old, and our hearing's not what it used to be. Not to mention everything sags, and swear to God, his farts turn to dust." She fanned herself off, and everyone fell into shock. It was comical. Harlow spit out her drink. Calista choked on hers.

Mel laughed hysterically, and Dee shook her head with a smile on her face as she patted Callie on the back.

It was a Sunday evening out with the girls at their favorite watering hole. The local pub-style restaurant where the Misfit gang frequently hung out.

"Dang, Mamma Deuce. I love that I never know what's going to come out of your mouth next. You're one of a kind, and that's one of the many things I adore about you." Mel raised her hand in the air for a high five. Which the old lady had no problem giving.

"I've got to keep you young ones on your toes somehow." Fanny winked, and Harlow smiled after she wiped her mouth.

"I envy what the two of you have, and I hope one day I find somebody special enough to grow old with, dust and all." Harlow winked back, and the proprietor laughed.

"You two are newer than these ones. I know Melody and Diamond well. Have for years now, but you..." Fanny shrugged her shoulders and gestured between Harlow and Calista. "Your names have escaped me."

"Harlow. My name is Harlow Ross. It's a pleasure to meet you." Harlow extended her hand to shake, and the old woman obliged.

"And I'm Calista Wyatt, but all of my friends call me Callie." Her friend gave a wave in greeting as well.

"It's nice to meet you two," Fanny said. She addressed Harlow next. "You're Toby's new girl.

I've heard so much about you. All great, of course." She rubbed her hands together with glee. "About time that boy got himself someone worthy again."

Harlow blushed. "Thank you."

"Speaking of the Misfit boss man, has anyone seen the finished tattoo yet? I've been dying to catch a glimpse." Calista looked at her expectantly. "Harlow has been wanting this for so long, and she finally took the leap."

"Well what are we waiting for?" Dee asked. "Stand up and show us the goods."

"Here?" Harlow looked around the semi-busy establishment.

Mel just gave her a "well, duh" look, and she took a deep breath.

Here goes nothing. Well, not nothing because the tattoo, it's everything. Okay, shut up, Har, and get on with it.

She lifted her shirt and looked down at the artwork she was in love with. "I can't wait to see it when all of the scabbing falls off, but it's kind of perfect, isn't it?"

"Holy shit. Yeah!" Dee exclaimed.

"There's nothing 'kind of' about it," Callie said. "It is absolutely perfect for you."

"Now that's some sexy work." Mel clapped her hands together.

"Bitchin'," Fanny chimed in, and Harlow couldn't agree more.

"You've got me curious. Who spilled the beans? Did Toby talk about Harlow with you? We want details," Mel said before Harlow had the chance. She had to admit, she was just as curious. She fixed her shirt and took a seat.

"You know how hard it is to get that boy to open up. Pshhh…" Fanny waved a hand in the air, as if to dismiss that thought. "It was your brother."

"Carson?" Mel did a double take. "Really?"

"Mm hm. The last few times he was in, he mentioned Toby got himself hooked up with a hot piece. Said she was a doctor and wrote for some fancy magazine. I was impressed. Also said she was a nice girl. Thought she was great for Toby. Hoped that his pal would take a chance and not fuck it up too bad. It's about time, too." Fanny reached across the table and took Harlow's hand. "He's a great catch, once you get through all the broken pieces. And, honey, I have a feeling, with all I heard and seeing you now, that you're sweet enough, smart enough, and strong enough to help him be whole again. Doesn't hurt that he's easy on the eyes." She fanned herself. "If only I were thirty years younger."

"That's for sure," Callie agreed, and she gave Harlow a sheepish smile. "What? Anyone with eyes can see Toby's gorgeous. That said, I also love that he's good to you and makes you happy."

Harlow nodded. "We're not making any promises right now. But he really does make me happy, and…" She took a deep breath. "I've already fallen hard for him."

"Glad to hear it." Dee squealed, and she hugged Mel, who smiled, and it lit up her whole face.

"For the record, I'm not a medical doctor. I'm a psychologist, and I write for *Twin City Women's Magazine*. My column is called Harlow Helps."

"Oh, I know. I checked you out as soon as Carson talked. Like I said earlier, I was quite impressed." Fanny stood. "Well, ladies, I'm afraid my break is up. Can I take your orders before I go?"

"We'll get our refills from Harold at the bar." Melody held up her beer. "We'd love a couple plates of nachos to share, if you're headed to the kitchen. Everyone okay with nachos?"

"Sounds good," Harlow replied as everyone else nodded their agreement. "Thank you, Fanny."

"Anything for my favorite girls." The older woman turned to walk away and stopped to look over her shoulder one last time. "See you in a bit."

"I guess it's fair to say my brother likes you. Both as a person, and at the thought of you with Toby. That's good," Melody said. Harlow turned from watching Fanny saunter away to look at her. "He's been tight with Toby a long time now, and I know Carson's opinion matters to Tob."

"Cheers." Harlow held up her glass of wine as the other three did the same with their drinks and took a sip. It was time for a subject change, and there was something bothering her. "I wanted to talk to you about something, actually."

"Uh oh. What's up?" Mel asked.

"Toby finally talked to me the other night, and I figured out he's your Mr. Idiosyncratic." Harlow gave her a wide-eyed stare as she tried not to divulge too much information. Dee and Calista looked between her and Mel like they were lost.

"That's huge!" Her friend got up to give her a hug and sat back down. "You know that, right? Toby doesn't talk to anyone."

"I figured out that much. Now I'm not sure what to do," Harlow admitted.

"Are you talking about the letter?" Dee asked. Harlow felt somewhat relieved that she knew as well. "Mel got me to read it when she originally planned to send it to the column."

"Letter? What letter?" Callie asked.

Mel saved her from having to explain further. "I've known Toby for a very long time. He's like family to me. A couple years ago, his fiancé died in a fire that trapped them both. He's been stuck inside his grief over what happened ever since. I was worried about him and wrote a letter to Harlow with my concerns. Instead of sending it in, I was able to give it to her in person, thanks to your introduction," she said. "I used a code name and called him Mr. Idiosyncratic to try and keep a little anonymity. Looks like it's all aired out now, since Toby shared his past with Harlow, and she now knows the letter was about him."

"Wow, that was a mouthful," Calista said. "What's the big deal about the letter?"

Harlow turned to look at her like she was crazy for not getting it. "The big deal is I feel like I should tell him about it. I'm afraid he might be upset that I knew about his tragedy, even though I wasn't sure it was about him at the time. Make sense?" She rubbed her temples. "I also can't say anything because Mel gave me the letter in confidence, and it'd be ethically wrong to break that trust."

"I honestly think you're worrying for nothing," Mel said. "I think it's great that he told you his story, but there's no reason Toby needs to know what I wrote to you. He'd probably just get really pissed off at me for it. I was worried. Now I look at him, and thanks to you, I see so much improvement. He never has to know about it. I know I won't say anything. So why would you?"

Harlow swallowed a lump in her throat. She had a bad feeling about this, but she also had to respect Melody's wishes, even if she disagreed. Her gut was still telling her to lay everything out. Instead of arguing her point, she gave in. "If that's what you feel is best. I guess I just felt guilty, like I'm withholding something from him. I don't want to betray his trust or yours."

"Everything will be okay. You'll see," Dee assured her. "Our lips are sealed."

"If you're sure." Harlow sighed. She mimicked zipping her mouth closed before throwing away an imaginary key. They knew her concerns, talked about them, and there was nothing more to be done for the time being but to move on. She took a deep breath in and slowly exhaled. There were a lot of good things going on in her life, and she wanted to count her blessings instead of worrying about the little things she couldn't change.

Chapter Twenty-Three

TOBY

Toby snorted the minute their Uber pulled up and he saw the neon sign. Leave it to Carson to find every strip club in the area. His buddy looked excited to be there, though, so he'd suck it up and try to have a good time. Since he'd met Harlow, a variety of tits and ass didn't have the same appeal as it used to. He had hers, and that's all he needed. She was the bright light in his dreary existence.

"Welcome to The Busy Beaver." Carson slapped him on the shoulder as they now stood near the entrance. The place seemed nice enough. The large brick building looked like it might have once been a warehouse of some sort once upon a time. It seemed to be newly renovated and classy enough.

Rebel laughed and rubbed his hands together as he strode to the entrance. "Well, what are we waiting for?"

"You coming in or what?" Carson waved him forward, and Toby took a deep breath of fresh air before he followed them inside.

"I've died and gone to heaven." Carson dramatically clutched his chest and stumbled backwards as they took in the establishment. Toby rolled his eyes. Lord knew he loved him like a brother, but he was a little over the top at times like these.

There was a long granite bar to the left of them, maybe six feet away. It was busy with both patrons and waitresses alike. Several tables and booths were situated to the right. They had a large stage going from one end of the place to the other like a catwalk, only with a pole. Then there was another section blocked by red velvet rope. The people in that area got extra attention, it seemed, and a bottle service. It made him wonder how much cash they had to fork over to sit there. Two bouncers stood by the entrance behind them—big, rough-looking dudes, too. They were muscle heads who looked like they'd taken a few too many steroids a time or two. There were more, of course, all over the place, but he couldn't care less. Toby continued to check the place out and spotted the champagne room, VIP section, as if the sign itself wasn't obvious. It was upstairs through a thick velvet curtain—the place where you got to have your own private show, if you had the extra cash. He figured if Carson got too annoying the way he was drooling and all, he might buy him some time in there, at some point, to catch a break.

"Dude," Rebel called out over the loud music and nudged his shoulder. "I think I see some seats over by the pool tables."

"You go grab them, and I'll get the first round." Toby tilted his head toward the bar and headed in that direction without waiting for a response.

The women were really working it tonight. He was approached no less than ten times or more in a five-minute time span for a dance. In the past, he would have been all over them, but he just wasn't feeling it tonight. They were gorgeous, but they weren't…her. His mind went back to Harlow, of course. They'd been spending a lot of time together, and he loved every minute of it. She was great, and he couldn't stop thinking about her, especially when they weren't together. He was fucked. Totally falling head over heels and enjoying it. Then there were times the guilt consumed him.

Damn it, James. Get your head on straight. Enjoy the night.

Of course, that only made him wonder how she was enjoying her night.

Shit!

"What can I get you, man?" the bartender asked.

Toby sighed. "Give me three Coors Light." He held up three fingers and placed some cash on the bar top.

"Tap or bottle?"

"Bottles." The guy nodded in his direction and took the cash with him. He returned a minute later with the three bottles of brew. "Keep the change."

With a nod, the bartender was on to the next person while Toby made his way to where his friends sat ogling the woman on stage.

"Big applause for Chantel, everyone," the MC announced.

The crowd cheered louder, and Rebel let out a loud whistle for the dancer who just finished her performance as she exited the stage. Toby smiled and sat back as the man on the loudspeaker continued to introduce the next act. The lights dimmed, and a lone spotlight shone bright in the direction of the entrance from backstage.

Ladies and gentlemen, please give a rowdy welcome to our very own Lacey! She's new, she's wild, and she's got all the right moves. Give it up!

A sexy silhouette stood still, waiting for the beat of the music to start up, before storming through the curtain that separated her from the rest of them. She was tall, she was stacked, and she was toned, with curves in all the right places. Toby could totally see the appeal, and yet she still had nothing on a certain brunette he couldn't wait to see again.

A pretty lace mask covered the top part of her face, and when the beat of Our Darkest Days' "Porn Star Dancing" began to play, he was in awe. This Lacey could really dance. Straight, long, blonde hair cascaded down her back as she ripped off her top hat and threw it into the crowd. The hollers, whistles, and cat calls were non-stop throughout. The white dress shirt she wore was the next to be ripped off as she sauntered forward like a woman on a mission. The top parts of her breasts bounced on top of her sheer bra, and her hips swayed to the beat. She exuded a sexy confidence he admired. Lacey's hands worked her body like magic, and damn, the woman was flexible. She bent forward and shimmied out of her shorts. It gave the men behind her a perfect view of her smooth round ass.

All that remained was her thong. Once she discarded her bottoms, she stepped back a few paces threw her leg up in the air and grabbed her ankle until it touched her ear. She held the position and twirled for everyone. It was quite the site to behold, and he was sure every cock in the vicinity was rock hard.

Carson spit out his beer, choked on it, and groaned. "Fuck me!" Toby smirked as his best friend scooted closer to the table. Carson leaned forward without taking his eyes off the very intriguing dancer. The man was mesmerized, and he couldn't blame him one bit.

Lacey pumped her hips and crawled sexily across the stage to accept a bit of the cash from the eager customers in pervert's row. When she reached the pole, she sat up, arched her back, and slid up to a standing position. Her legs wrapped around it, and she climbed to the top. She spun herself around and round, flipped herself upside down, and stretch out as she hung on backwards. Her smile was radiant, and her body was slick.

"Holy crap. Look at that," Rebel said. The guy rubbed his eyes and did a double take. Toby smirked and took a chug of the bottle in front of him. The amber liquid went down smoothly, and he wasn't sure which he was enjoying more: the performance on stage or watching the two knuckleheads beside him completely entranced. He'd known each for a while now. Carson for longer, of course, and he couldn't recall the last time a woman seemed to affect them like this.

"I call dibs, you fuckers." Carson gulped. "I

think I'm in love."

Rebel snorted, and Toby chuckled. "Fine with me. I'm into Harlow anyway."

"Glad to hear it." Rebel winked then addressed Carson. "Good luck with that. I bet every guy in here feels the same way."

Carson flipped him off, and Toby shook his head. The song was coming to an end. Lacey reached up to grip the bar and twirled herself back down the pole. Once her feet were secure on the stage, she did a complete body flip and landed gracefully with her arms in the air. She blew the entire establishment a kiss for her finale.

It was a fucking epic performance, and the bar went wild with applause.

"I've got to see if I can get a lock on some time with the lovely Lacey." Carson abruptly stood and went in search of someone who worked there to get his dance. Rebel's shoulders shook with laughter, and Toby rolled his eyes.

"Damn, Reb. Never thought I'd see the day. Carson's already hooked."

"It'll be fun to see how this plays out. Got a feeling our boy's going to be a regular from now on until he gets this chick out of his system." Rebel grinned and shook his head as if in disbelief. "Want to play some pool?"

"Sounds good, brother. Go wrack them up." Toby followed Rebel to one of the vacant pool tables and kicked some ass at it for the most part. It wasn't long before Carson joined them, sulking.

"She's not available for a private dance. What kind of bullshit is that?"

Toby shrugged. "Don't know man. Want to play the winner?" He gestured to the pool table.

Rebel gave him a chin lift, and soon, the entertainment was put to the back of everyone's mind. They enjoyed the game, each other's company, and the drinks they slugged back. It turned out to be a good night, after all.

Chapter Twenty-Four

Dear Harlow:

Why do good things always come to an end? I just got dumped. We were together a year and a half, and he left me for my sister, of all people. I'm so hurt and angry I'd just love to kick both their A$$@$. So, while I take a deep breath and remind myself I look horrible in orange, I'm at a loss on how to proceed.

I did throw all his crap to the curb, him included. And my sister, well, she can kiss my...I'll leave that to your imagination. Have you ever had this type of situation happen on the column before? Any tips to get through it?

The man, I can get over eventually. The jerkoff told me he was sleeping with her while we were on an intimate dinner date. Like a sucker, I thought I was there because he was going to propose. Boy was I wrong.

168

Do you think I'll be able to salvage the relationship with my sister one day? Sadly, we used to be so close, but as it stands, it doesn't feel like I'll ever be able to forgive her betrayal. Help!

If anything, it was just nice to vent, and let's face it, I cried too.

~Hopeless, Hurt, and Betrayed in Minneapolis~

*

Dear Hopeless, Hurt, and Betrayed:

First, I believe your Prince Charming is out there. I'm sure of it. It just takes some of us longer to find him than others.

Secondly, some good things come to an end because they just weren't meant to be. Unfortunately, we get cheating stories written in often. They don't get any easier, and there is no right answer or tips to follow. You did the right thing by getting rid of him as soon as you could. The man sounds like a real loser, and you deserve better.

It's always best to know your self-worth.

Thirdly, as for your sister, that's a tough one that only you can answer. She isn't worthy of your trust or your time, but who knows what the future holds for you both? It could

change.

In the meantime, cry some more, scream, or punch a pillow to get out those frustrations to make you feel better. And always know you can write in anytime to vent, as you put it. I'm happy to lend you an ear.

Big Hugs,
Harlow

***

HARLOW

Time flew by as summer turned into fall. Harlow and Toby had been together for a couple of months now. It was confusing trying to label what they were. Toby warned her he wasn't sure he could deal with a serious relationship from the beginning, but as time went on, she couldn't help but want the commitment. She was his, regardless, and Harlow knew without a doubt that she loved him wholeheartedly. Scars and all. Just as she suspected he was in denial and might love her too.

It was a chilly October evening, and Harlow pulled the lapels of her jacket closer together against the wind as she walked down Main Street. She was meeting up with Toby at St. Anthony's Main Theater for their date. "Sorry I'm late," she said, leaning forward on the tips of her toes so she could give him a kiss. "What are we seeing?"

"In the spirit of this time of year, I figured we could see *Halloween*. You can't beat the classics."

Toby grinned. "Feel free to get as close as possible if you get scared."

"Hm, I just might," she said. "I've seen all of the old ones. Let's just hope this new one is just as good as the rest. Can you believe it's been, like, forty years since the original came out on the big screen?"

"That just makes me feel like I'm getting old when you put it that way." Toby chuckled as he handed her a ticket to get in. "It came out a little before my time, but like you, I've still seen them all."

"Okay, then." Harlow giggled. "Come on, old man. I need some popcorn."

"I'll show you old," Toby said. Harlow squealed in delight as he lifted her up and spun her around.

"Okay, okay." Harlow held onto him as he put her down and enjoyed his comforting embrace for a moment longer. "My man's not old at all. He's a thirty-three-year-old sexy, manly man. Big, tough, and talented. Now can I have my popcorn?"

"Your man, huh?" Toby winked. "I like the sound of that."

Heck yeah! Well, okay then.

Harlow smirked as Toby grabbed her hand and led the way to the concession stand. It was such a good start to the night. She couldn't wait for the rest and decided tonight was the night she was going to tell him the depth of her feelings. She just hoped it didn't backfire.

"Just one more thing before the movie starts," Harlow said. They had their popcorn and jumbo drinks on hand and had just sat down in the packed theater. "Scared or not, I want to be close to you, Toby. Will you hold me later, if I need it?"

"Oh, baby." Toby leaned in closer. "I'll hold you, kiss you, touch you…" The lights dimmed, and the movie began when Toby showed her with one hell of a kiss that left her breathless.

Almost two hours later, they were back outside again, walking hand in hand and on their way to Harlow's place. Her apartment was closer than his to the theater.

"So how was your dinner with Calista?" Toby asked. Calista had called Harlow earlier in the day asking for a little girl time to talk about a few issues she was having. Which was why she'd met Toby at the theater instead of going with him from the start.

"It went well, considering. She's got a lot on her mind right now with work. She's thinking of leaving the restaurant and opening up her own catering business."

Toby whistled. "It's good to have goals. I hope it all works out for her, then."

"Yeah, me too," Harlow said. "She's been working at Caliente for the last four years as a sous chef and loving it. But now there's a new owner, and from what I hear, he's a real piece of work. Calista is such a strong person, a hard worker, and she's resilient, so I have no doubt she'll succeed at whatever she puts her mind to. I'm not very worried at this point."

"Caliente? I've never been." Toby shrugged. "What kind of restaurant is it?"

"It's an upscale place with French-inspired cuisine. I've only been once myself, to tell you the truth, when Calista started there. It's good food but really hard on the wallet." Harlow smiled. "I could take you there sometime, if you'd like."

"I'd go anywhere with you, babe," Toby said.

"Aw, look." Harlow pointed across the street toward an elderly couple. The old man was helping his wife down some building steps. "They're as cute together as Fanny and Dusty. Don't you think? That's the type of love I hope to find some day—everlasting."

Toby looked confused. "Who?"

"Who what?" It was Harlow's turn now.

"You said Fanny and Dusty. I don't know anybody named Dusty, and last time I checked, Mamma Deuce was a happily married woman." Toby's eyebrow arched.

"Well, she is." Harlow blushed. "I just forgot his name. Last time I went to Fanny's with the girls, she joined us for a bit. When she sat down for her break, she told us, and I quote: 'Damn, I love that man, but we're getting old and our hearing's not what it used to be. Not to mention everything sags, and swear to God his farts turn to dust.' I just figured I'd call her husband Dusty until we were formally introduced."

Toby guffawed, and she loved it. It was a full, hearty laugh from deep in his belly, and her chest felt like it swelled with pride for helping him with that. He needed to smile and laugh more.

"Holy shit!" Toby wiped his eyes. "His name's Harold, babe. Fanny's husband is Harold. I don't think I've laughed that hard in years."

Harlow stopped and pulled him to a halt with

her. She reached up and cupped the sides of his face. "Happy is a good look for you. You deserve this and so much more. I hope you realize that because I sometimes wonder."

"Yes, thanks to you," Toby said. He wrapped his arms around her until she was flush against him for a kiss. The wind picked up, and she shivered, but it wasn't until the downpour of rain fell on top of them that they broke apart breathlessly. Harlow laughed, and Toby smiled as she stepped back tipped her head up and twirled around the wet sidewalk.

"This moment feels magical. Don't you think?" she asked. "I feel so elated. Typical autumn weather be damned." Harlow picked that moment to jump into a puddle and dance in the rain.

Toby chuckled. "Come here, crazy woman, before you get yourself sick." Toby held out his hand and pulled her close again as soon as she reached for him. He pressed his forehead to hers and just breathed her in. She loved it. Her hair was plastered to her face, and fat drops of water dripped off his. "As much as I love to see you so happy and carefree like this, I think it's time to get out of the cold. I'll take you home, then you can let me love you properly."

"An offer I'd never refuse," Harlow replied. She gripped his hand tighter and led the way as they ran the few last remaining blocks to her apartment complex.

***

TOBY

The minute they walked in, Toby slammed the door closed with his foot and pressed her against the wall to devour her mouth. He needed her, couldn't ever get enough, and at times, it drove him crazy. To want someone this much was just insane, but there, he was feeling it. They tore at each other's clothes. It took a bit of effort seeing as they were soaked from the rain. Instead of running like a normal person would when the downpour started, Harlow had embraced it. She'd danced in the rain for him like he used to as a kid, and fuck was it ever nice to be carefree for once. She did that to him. Made him want to be a better man. To enjoy life again. She was a lifeline for him after feeling like he'd been drowning for so long. It was like he could finally breathe again. Damn it, and now he was thinking nonsense. He grunted when he finally got her shirt off and dropped to his knees so he could work on her jeans. "I've got to take you here, hard and fast, then we'll go slow, I promise." He looked up past her heaving chest to see her nodding eagerly, as if she felt the same way, and he smirked. He yanked her underwear at the same time he shimmied her pants down her legs and cursed when her clothes got caught on her shoes.

Christ!

When she was finally free, he stood up and threw each article behind him. Toby took just enough time to unzip, pull his dick out, and enter her in one smooth stroke to the hilt. He just didn't have the patience for his own clothes right then. The pull was too strong. Harlow's legs wrapped around his waist as he furiously thrust into her over and over. He could swear nothing ever felt as good as this, as she did when they were joined. That thought alone normally scared the shit out of him. Harlow threw her head back and moaned. Her nails dug into his shoulders. It was a move she did often, and she ran them down his back as she held on for the ride. Her fingers trailed back up into his hair, gripping hard, and she directed him back to her mouth. The minute her soft lush mouth met his, she opened for him. Their tongues touched, caressed, and tasted. Her hips moved to meet his, matching his frenzied pace. He knew it wasn't going to last much longer. Her pussy was so wet, warm, and smooth, tight, and it fit him like he was made to be there. "So close." Toby trembled. "Come for me. Let me feel it before I let go."

"Kay." Harlow nodded. She licked the index finger on her left hand and moved it between them to reach between her legs and play with her clit. She rubbed in circles slowly at first and then faster the more she got worked up.

"Fucking sexy," Toby growled and slammed in faster.

Harlow cried out. "Yes, almost there, almost— holy shit, Toby! Toby!" The minute she gushed, hell, the second he felt her pulse, he erupted until he was weak in the knees. His forehead was pressed against the hallway wall as he tried to catch his breath, and Harlow rubbed his back to give him a minute.

"You okay?" She gave him a quick kiss on the

side of his head before he straightened to look at her.

"Never better." He smiled and squeezed her ass as he carried her to her bedroom while they were still joined. "It's not every day I'm left breathless and in need of a minute before I can move again. He winked, and she giggled.

"You say the nicest things," she teased and laughed out loud as she bounced on the bed when he dropped her in the middle of it.

"Do I?" Toby shook his head and finally got undressed. She amused him. He liked that they could be playful before, during, and after making love. It was refreshing.

Harlow nodded. "Let's take a nap before round two. I'm feeling a little tired."

"Anything for you, babe." He leaned over to kiss her on the forehead and pulled the covers back before joining in. She was on her side, and he closed the distance to spoon with her. His front to her back, she grabbed his hand to hold and placed it near her heart. It was quiet, blissfully so. Minutes had passed, and just as he was about to fall asleep, Harlow being Harlow kept him on his toes and surprised him.

"Toby?" she whispered. "Are you still awake?"

"Hm," he mumbled.

"I love you."

Unbeknownst to Harlow, his eyes popped open. She wiggled a bit as if to get comfortable, and her breathing evened out before he could think to respond. Unlike the woman in his arms, sleep eluded him. Those three words were game changing, as much as he liked hearing them.

There was no doubt Harlow was an amazing woman, and there were feelings; he felt them for her, knew without a doubt he wanted her in his life. There hadn't been another woman since they got together. He didn't want anyone else.

But to have her love me?

He knew if he gave into his heart, it would just make him feel guilty, and he had to figure out how to get past it.

He owed it to them both so they could keep what they'd built together.

Chapter Twenty-Five

Dear Harlow:

I've been good friends with this guy for about four years now. He's my brother's roommate, who we'll call Jack, and lately, I've been feeling more than I should for him. Last weekend, we were drinking and hooked up for the first time. It was amazing, and I can't stop thinking about it. I don't know what to do. Should I lay it all out there and see if he feels the same? Or should I try to move on? We have the same group of friends, and I'm afraid to ruin what we already have. I don't want to lose him, either way. Help!

~Confused and Crushing in Minneapolis~

*

Dear Confused and Crushing:
Some of the best relationships start off with

being friends first before starting something more. Talk to Jack. I'm sure it was just as amazing for him as it was for you. There is nothing wrong with giving in to your urges every now and again. Communication is key here, and I say, lay it all out there. You may have regrets later if you don't.

Worst case scenario, he doesn't reciprocate your feelings, and you remain friends. Best case, your desires are met, he feels the same way, and you all live happily ever after.

I'm rooting for you.

All my best,

Harlow

***

HARLOW

The pitter patter of heavy rain drops against the bedroom window woke Harlow. She stretched with a smile on her face as she thought about the night before. The movie, playing in the rain, and Toby taking her hard against the wall. He'd woken her periodically through the night for some more sexy times too, and she felt well and truly loved. It was amazing.

The soft cotton of Toby's shirt caressed her body as her back arched in a stretch. She threw her arms above her head and moaned before she opened her eyes fully. The sight of her delectable tattooist sitting up beside her in bed was what greeted her. And what a sight to behold. He was half naked, nothing on but his jeans open at the fly. He looked completely relaxed with a coffee in one hand and a piece of paper he was reading in the other.

"Hey, handsome. You been up long?"

"About an hour." He gripped the paper tighter and gave her a look she didn't quite understand. "Figured I'd let you sleep a bit more, make some coffee, and I'd relax a little seeing as I took the day off to spend it with you. Funny how plans can change in a split second, though, huh?"

"Excuse me? Forgive me for being a little confused here, but I just woke up. What's wrong?" It wasn't necessarily what he said, it was more about his body language. Something had changed in his demeanour from last night to this morning, and whatever it was, it wasn't good. He looked hurt, maybe even a little pissed off at her.

"Do you have anything you want to tell me?" Toby put his mug down on the ground and waited for her to respond.

Harlow sat up. "I don't know. Should I?"

"What the fuck, Harlow. You knew!" He waved the paper around and shoved it in her face. "Here I was agonizing over telling you about my past with Carley, and you already fucking knew about it, with this. I trusted you. Do you have any idea how hard that was for me? To move on and be with you."

"I-I didn't know at first." She got on her knees to plead when he sprang up from his seat to pace in front of the bed. She reached out for him, but he brushed her off, and she could feel the moment her heart broke. It was beating so hard, it felt like it was about to be ripped right from her chest at any moment. Tears sprang to her eyes. "Please let me explain."

"Then talk," he said. He sounded exasperated with her. "Who the fuck wrote this? Was it made public? You put it in your column?"

"Where did you find that?" Harlow bit her lip to keep from sobbing. She'd never seen him this upset.

"Really? That's your first question. I can't believe this shit." Toby sat down abruptly on the side of the bed and put on his socks. "Word to the wise, Harlow. You try to keep something from someone, you don't leave it out in the open. The letter was on the damn counter beside your other mail. Saw it while I was making my coffee."

She remembered then. She'd taken the letter out of her purse the other night, debating on whether she should just get rid of it. She'd meant to after her talk with Mel a little while ago but then forgot about it. When she was with Toby, they mostly went to his place. Rarely did they come to her apartment. Only they had last night because it was closer.

Harlow nodded in acknowledgement. "I received the letter before we even met from someone who was worried about you. As a favor to them, I never made it public. I promise you, it never made it in Twin City. It was only after you told me what happened that I realized this letter was about you. Toby, I swear it. I know you're upset but…"

"Who?" He turned his head sideways to look at her again, and this time, her sob escaped. He looked so haunted, defeated, and betrayed. She couldn't stand it.

"I-I can't tell you." It came out as a whisper, and she winced. Her response sounded bad, even to her own ears. "I'm sorry, but I have an ethical responsibility to keep my source confidential."

"Well, fuck you and your ethics." Toby jumped up again, buttoned up his pants, and pointed an accusing finger in her direction. He looked her up and down with a curl of his lip and snarled. "Keep my shirt. I don't want it, or you, for that matter."

"You don't mean that." Harlow quickly followed as he charged out of her bedroom. "I can understand that you might need time to think about all of this, but I didn't do anything wrong. I would never intentionally hurt you. I love you, Toby, and I haven't loved anyone since before Lily died. You're the first person I've been with since. The first person who understood what I really went through when I lost her. Take some time, but don't shut me out. We're good together." She wiped the tears that were clouding her vision, and Toby looked anguished.

"It's too late," he replied, wiping some moisture from his own eyes. "I warned you I didn't think I had forever in me anymore. Why do you think I didn't say I loved you back? I heard you last night, and I'm hearing you now. Forget about us. Better yet, forget about me. As you can see, I'm damaged goods."

"Don't you dare say that." Harlow was at her snapping point now. She had to get through to him before he walked out. As it stood, he was zipping up his jacket and putting on his shoes to leave. He'd be out the door in a minute. "You were right. It is too late because you're amazing, Toby, whether you want to see it in yourself or not. I could never forget you or what we have. You're the one throwing it away, so that's on you. I just hope it's not too late when you realize what a mistake you've made by walking out that door."

"At this point, it's a chance I'll have to take," he said. He yanked open the door and looked over his shoulder. "You should have told me. Trust is not something I give lightly."

By the time Toby walked out, Harlow was shaking. She collapsed in a heap in the same hallway they'd made love in the night before. She was heartbroken, utterly devastated by his reaction, and she cursed him for his stubborn ways. She should have known better.

Toby was obviously stuck in the past, not ready to move on, no matter how much patience she gave him or how much she'd tried to help him feel better. This morning had been an eye opener, and she was beginning to lose hope.

How was she ever supposed to compete with a ghost?

They had been doomed from the start.

Chapter Twenty-Six

TOBY

As soon as the door shut behind him, he banged his head against it. He could hear Harlow sobbing from inside, and it tore him apart. He just felt so violated, and his anger got the best of him. He needed to leave and cool down, but first, he was going to get to the bottom of this. That letter bugged him, and he was determined to find out who wrote it. It was clearly from someone who knew him well. That left only about a handful of people, and they all needed to mind their own fucking business. Let him live his own life. He finally had a good woman again, but she was better off without him. Wasn't she?

Shit!

Toby yanked at his hair and walked away while he still could. His heart ached, but he'd brought that on himself. He should be used to it by now. After hailing a cab, he phoned Misfit, and Diamond answered. "Misfit Tattoo, Dee speaking. How may I help you?"

"It's me," he said. "We need a meeting, and I'll need everyone present for it. I'll be at the shop in that hour we close for lunch. There are things that need to be said, and I don't want to repeat myself. We clear?"

"Crystal. Everything all right?" Dee asked.

Toby was quick to reply. "I'll be there soon enough, and you'll find out."

"Whoa," she said. "Okay, then. I'll let everyone know we're having lunch in the break room today. Anything else, boss?"

Toby sighed. "No, I'll see you soon, Dee."

"Uh huh. Soon," she replied before hanging up.

As he disconnected, Toby rubbed a hand down his face and pocketed his phone. He looked out the cab's window to the blurry sites of the city he loved, and he already knew it was going to be a long-ass day ahead.

When he made it home, he went straight upstairs to take a shower and grab a beer before confronting his friends. There was some time to kill, and it was five o'clock somewhere in the world. Today, he needed it.

When he woke up this morning, the plans he'd made with Harlow had held so much promise. He'd wanted to spend all of it with her, from sun up to sun down. Show her with actions what he had a hard time saying with words, about how much he cared. Only because of hurt feelings and pride, he'd ended their relationship instead. He kept telling himself it was easier this way. He was so fucked up. He didn't deserve her, anyway. Toby's hands fisted at his sides, and he took a few deep breaths to calm down. One beer turned into two before he headed into Misfit for the confrontation.

When he got there, Carson was waiting in the lobby. They put a **'BE BACK IN AN HOUR'** sign on the door and locked up. "Hey, man. Everyone's waiting for us in the break room."

True to his word, when he walked in with Carson, everyone was sitting at the table, eating pizza. They all looked up when they saw him and quieted down.

Rebel gave him a nod in acknowledgement, Dee waved, Carson grabbed himself a slice, and Mel was the first one to speak up. "What's up, Tob? Are you okay?"

"No, I'm not okay, so I'll get to it. Harlow and I are done. I just ended it this morning. You probably won't be seeing her around much anymore. I know some of you are friends with her, and what you do on your own time is your business." He shrugged and leaned against the wall, pretending he wasn't affected by this news in the least. It was a crock of shit, but they didn't need to know that. He was pissed off; that's what they needed to see. "She lied to me and is protecting one of you while doing it."

"What the fuck?" Carson sat up.

"Are you serious?" Rebel folded his arms across his chest. "Letting that woman go would be the dumbest thing you've ever done," he grumbled.

Toby ignored him. "Who wrote the letter?" He watched each of them closely. Carson and Rebel looked confused, if not a little disappointed in him. Dee's eyes went wide, and Mel stayed quiet. He had his answer. As suspected, it was one of the girls. He should have known it'd be between those two.

He pointed at Dee. "Was it you?" He stood up straighter and took a step toward her. Shockingly, he was interrupted from his interrogation when Melody's chair fell over with a loud crash, and she rushed out of the room. He watched her go then gave Diamond the stink eye. "Talk!"

"It wasn't me, but I knew about it." She lifted her chin in defiance. "You've been destructive for a long time now, Toby, and we were all worried. Especially when you shut most of us out. Did you read it? Because what was said was nothing horrible, and it never went public. Only a few people have seen it. Me, Harlow, and Mel. I'll tell you one thing, though, Rebel's right. You are a dumbass if you left Harlow because of this. That woman loves you, and until this moment, it was nice to see you happy again."

"Do I look happy to you?" he roared, back on the defensive. "You have no idea what I went through or how it felt after Carley died. I was crushed, and it's not a situation you just get over. Is it?" He exhaled loudly. "Harlow lied to me about it when I told her. She already knew and didn't tell me shit that she did. I trusted her. Then, this morning, I find it on her counter, and she didn't have the decency to tell me who even wrote the thing. She refused to tell me!"

Dee flinched in her spot as his yelling got louder. Toby's face was red, and a vein throbbed in his forehead.

"It was me, you idiot." Mel charged up to him,

and he spun around to face her. "Now sit your ass down for your own good and hear me out."

"I'm good right here." Toby narrowed his eyes and folded his arms while everyone else looked at their standoff.

"Whatever." Melody threw her hands in the air. "You read the original letter I gave to Harlow, but you never read her response." She threw Harlow's written words at him, and he bent to pick them up. "Now, listen to me, Toby James. She didn't know it was you when I gave her the letter. I never used your real name. When Harlow finally figured it out, she confronted me and all but begged me to let her come clean. I didn't think it was a big deal and brushed her off. That was my mistake, and I'll own up to it. She couldn't tell you because it goes against the grain. She's a psychologist, for Christ's sake. She got her degree from Stanford. Haven't you ever heard of doctor-patient confidentiality? I know she works for the magazine now, but the same ethics apply, Toby. I wrote the letter; therefore, she needed my permission to tell you. She treated my situation, or should I say *yours,* as if I was in her shrink's chair. The person you should be mad at is me." She pointed at her chest and closed any remaining distance between them.

"Oh, I'm pissed off." Toby pointed his finger at her this time. "You had no right."

"I was worried!" Mel screamed. "You were on a downward spiral. You were wearing yourself out and wouldn't listen to anybody. You had a different woman almost every night, worked more than you slept, and you barely ate. If I had known you were about to fall for Harlow and get your stubborn head out of your ass, maybe I wouldn't have done anything, but I'm not psychic. We're more than friends, Toby, more than boss and employee. You're my family. It might not be by blood, but you're still my brother, and I love you, so smarten up and do it fast. We've all had enough of this shit, and you're using it as an excuse to push away the woman you're crazy about."

"I know what I feel. I don't need you to tell me, and it's easier said than done." Toby sulked. By the time Mel stopped yelling at him, it was as if the fight had suddenly left him. "You're still on my shit list."

Mel rolled her eyes, threw her hands in the air again, and slammed the door shut behind her as she left the room.

Carson stood, slowly approached Toby, and clapped his friend on the shoulder. "All right, brother, why don't we take a breather? I think you should go home, read that response, and we'll take it one day at a time until we can get past all this. But do me a favor and think on it hard so you can come to the right decision. Get your woman back. She's the real deal, and I envy you that. The one-night stands get old, man. Reach for your happy and hold on tight. She's worth it. You know it, and despite what you think, you deserve it. This is for keeps."

Toby sighed. He'd read it and think about what Carson said, but first, he needed another drink to ease the pain of betrayal he still felt.

Chapter Twenty-Seven

Dear Readers:

It's been awhile since the roles were reversed, and today is one of those days. I love when you write in every week. Helping people has always been a passion of mine. It's rewarding, and I'd like to thank you all for the support you give to both me and this column. Only for this article, I'm giving you me again.

A few months back, I was introduced to a group of really great people, and they fast became my friends. We'll call them Rae, Parker, Tyler, Romeo, and James. You see, Lily's birthday was coming up, and I wanted to get a tattoo, my very first in her honor. Not only that but the placement would also cover some of the physical scars left on me from the accident. I had this idea that it would turn my ugly into something beautiful again, just like my little girl was.

I met Tyler first at a dinner with my best friend. Tyler worked at this highly sought-after tattoo parlor and convinced me to come check it out, so I wouldn't chicken out.

Tyler's a fan of Harlow Helps, and she asked me to look at a letter she wrote, but she was nervous about sharing it publicly. She was worried about someone she cared for, and as a favor, I decided to keep it private. I promised her I'd have a look and that I'd reply with a letter of my own when we met up again. It seemed simple enough.

This letter, although written with good intentions, turned out to be about someone I came to love.

It was when I went to the tattoo parlor that I met James for the first time.

I was there to meet Tyler, but she was busy with a client, and it was just me and James up front. There was an instant magnetism that I've never felt before, and he was so nice, in personality and to look at. We talked about the tattoo I wanted, and James took it upon himself to make my dream into a reality. He drew my idea and then later gave me the most beautiful tattoo I could imagine. He's that good of an artist.

That same night, I ran into Romeo, Tyler's twin brother. He's an adorable man who can make anyone laugh with his cheesy pick-up lines and easy-going persona. A man you can't help but like.

A few days later, I was introduced to Rae, a vivacious woman with a big personality, and Parker, a broody bad boy with a heart of gold. For the first time in a long time, my life was looking up, and all because these five people welcomed me into their group with open arms.

Since my daughter died, I became a loner by choice, and I never realized how lonely I'd become.

James was a kindred spirit. He understood me, unlike anyone else I met, because he suffered from his own loss and knew grief as well as I did.

Our relationship grew, and we couldn't fight the attraction for much longer. He's someone so special, with a tremendous talent for drawing and inking skin. He's caring and thoughtful, and we had so much in common from our love of motorcycles to old-school horror movies. It didn't take long before I fell in love, despite his warning that he wasn't sure he could let himself feel the same.

He had his reasons, and they were good ones. I'll leave it at that.

So, what's the reason for my rant, you might ask?

I owe him a heartfelt apology, and I'm hoping this post reaches him. Our complicated relationship has unfortunately come to an end. I unintentionally hurt him, and I have to try to make amends.

Mr. James, if you're reading this, I am truly sorry. You bared your heart and soul to me, told me things about you that not a lot of people are privy to, and I didn't tell you that I already knew because I didn't know how. I hope you can find it in your heart to one day forgive me.

All my love,

XO

Harlow

***

HARLOW

Almost a week had gone by since Toby stormed out of her life and she had shut everyone out again. She just needed time to put herself back together before facing the world. Calista called repeatedly, as well as Mel and Dee. Heck, Carson and Rebel even tried to check in. She just needed time. She'd made herself whole once before. She could do it again...eventually.

Her heartbreak turned into anger after a few days, then the anger turned into exhaustion. Damn Toby for being so stubborn when she hadn't done anything wrong.

Men! Pftt...

God, they're a complicated species.

Harlow felt so pathetic, she'd even checked out old Blank Canvas reruns, Toby's former reality TV show, just to see him again. Torturing herself whenever Carley and Toby were in an episode together. They looked great as a couple too, but she had enough.

The walls of her apartment felt like they were closing in on her, and she had to escape. During her outing, she found herself in front of her daughter's marked grave. The fresh air was crisp, the sky an overcast of grey just like her mood, and it was chilly out. "Hey, baby," she said. Harlow bent down to clear some of the colorful leaves and debris from Lily's tombstone. "I miss you so much, I ache with it. I don't think the feeling will ever go away, but I was so lucky to be your mommy while I could. I don't want you to ever forget that I love you. I know somehow that you're here with me, even though I can't see you. You're in my heart, Lily Jane." Harlow's knees gave out, and she sat on the cold grass. "It's been a few months since I've visited, and I'm sorry for not coming to you sooner. I recently met a group of great people who became friends, thanks to your Aunty Calista. They helped get me out of my shell and out of the house more often. They're a great bunch. I'm sure you would have adored them. Then Mommy had to go and fall in love. His name is Toby. I wasn't expecting it, baby, but it happened quickly and with a bang. I think you would have probably fallen just as hard, and I bet he'd make a great daddy someday." She wiped a tear from her cheek and sighed with regret. "Unfortunately, it didn't work out, and he's mad at me. He has his own issues, and who knows, maybe I'm just destined to be alone. I'll have to learn to live with that, accept it, but I'll be okay. Life goes on. One day at a time." Her shoulders shook as she silently cried. "I hurt, baby girl, and I'm tired." She pressed her fingers against her lips as she hiccupped and lowered her face into her hands. "What I wouldn't give to have you back here with me. I got a tattoo in your memory. It's beautiful. In my heart and in my mind, I'll always cherish the time we had. One day, we'll meet again, and I can look upon your beautiful smile, see that adorable dimple in your chubby little cheek, and hold you in my arms." Harlow collapsed forward on top of her daughter's grave, oblivious to anything or anyone around her. She'd started the day sad about Toby and ended it with her daughter, vowing to visit again one day soon.

***

CALISTA

Harlow had been avoiding her, and she'd had enough of the silent treatment. She was worried, they all were, ever since Toby's stunt the other day. Out of respect, they'd all given her a few days like she wanted. Callie had talked to Mel and Dee earlier, and the plan was for her to spend some one on one time with her bestie, so they could slowly

196

get her to the land of the living again. They were having a girl's night, whether Harlow wanted one or not. She wasn't answering her phone or the door, so Calista got out her key—the one Harlow gave to her in case of emergency. She just happened to think today was emergency enough. Operation Harlow Heartbreak to Happiness was a go, step one in progress. The door banged against the hallway wall as she barged into the quiet apartment. "Harlow, it's rise and shine time."

Calista walked by the empty kitchen and living room. She took a quick peek in the bathroom and saved the bedroom for last. "Time to get up." She'd automatically assumed that she might be napping, but apparently, she wasn't home. "Hm," Callie blew some hair out of her eye and checked the time on her cell before she texted Mel.

Calista: She's not home. I'm going to stick around for a bit until she gets here.

Melody: K, keep us posted. We'll meet up same time as planned. I got the booze, Dee has the junk food covered. We're golden.

An hour passed by in a blur, then two, and it was getting dark out. No matter how many times she tried to call Harlow, there was no answer, and she was beginning to worry. This was so unlike her.

Callie called Mel first, and she picked up on the second ring.

"Hey, have you heard from her? I've got nothing, and I'm starting to worry."

"I wish," Melody said. "Hang tight. I'll call Dee and see if she's heard anything. We were supposed to meet up in a few anyway and head over to Harlow's for girl's night. It's probably a long shot, but you never know. If that doesn't pan out, I'll call in the guys, see if we can figure out a plan to find her."

"Thanks, Mel. I'll stay here, let you know if anything changes, and try to think of places she might be. Call me back soon as you can."

***

MELODY

"Dee, we have a situation. Calista can't get a hold of Harlow. She's not home and not answering her cell. It's getting dark, and this is not our girl's norm. Calista's getting worried, which is getting me worked up too."

"Whoa," Dee said. "First off, take a deep breath. I'm leaving now. Meet you at her place with Calista. You want to call the guys for some help with this, or should I?"

"The more people looking, the better. I'll call Carson. You try Rebel," Mel replied. "Then I'll get a hold of Toby. He's an ass, and I'm still upset, but I know he cares, and he'll want in on this."

"Got it. See you shortly."

"Right." Mel hung up and raced to get her jacket. She was just locking up her door when she got a hold of Carson.

"Hello, you've reached Carson Tyler. Best

brother, God's gift to women, and number one tattooist. How can I help you?"

"Yeah, right." Mel snorted. "Are you available?"

Carson chuckled. "Oh, how you wound me, baby sister."

"You're only older by three minutes. Now listen up, chucklehead, I'm going to need you and the rest of the guys to meet us at Harlow's place. Dee's calling Rebel now. I'll have to call Toby when I'm done with you. Calista went over to her place this afternoon to talk her into a girl's night, only she wasn't home, and that was hours ago. We still can't find her. It's getting dark. It's cold out, and there's no answer on her phone."

"Okay, hold on a minute. I'm with Rebel and Toby right now at his place, and it looks like he's filling Toby in—"

"Mel, what the fuck? Is she okay? Tell me she's good." Toby sounded panicked. "I'm putting my shoes on right now." The phone shuffled, and she could hear him talk to her brother. "Lock up and meet me there. I'm taking the bike. It's faster."

"I'm calling because I don't know, Tob. Calm down and meet us in one piece. Calista's thinking of places she might be, in the meantime, then we'll go search if she isn't home yet. Capiche?" Mel slammed her car door shut and started the engine. "See you in a few, yeah?"

"Fuck, Mel, I'm going out of my mind." Toby cleared his throat. "Yeah," he said before he hung up. And, right then and there, Mel knew there was hope yet for the troubled couple. But first, they needed to find the missing piece.

Chapter Twenty-Eight

Dear Harlow:

How do you make it up to someone after you've made a stupid mistake?

I met this amazing woman, but as soon as she told me she loved me, I freaked out and ended our relationship. I let those words scare me off and took the coward's way out. I wasn't ready to face how much I loved her in return.

~Sincerely, Once Burned~

*

Dear Once Burned:

That makes me wonder what made you finally decide you were ready to admit you love her back?

Sounds to me like you need to communicate with a few people. The woman you love, for one. Talk to her, explain why you were scared, and it probably wouldn't hurt to give her a grand gesture to prove you won't pull that stunt again

I know what it's like to be in this situation. It hurts something fierce, but if she loves you like you claim she does, I'm sure it'll all work out in the end.

Now, the next person you should think about talking to is a trained professional. There are clearly underlying issues that made you freak out, to begin with, and you need to work through that. This way, you can have a healthy relationship going forward.

Feel free to email me and I'd be happy to give you a list of resources.

Best of luck,
Harlow

***

TOBY

"What the hell is he doing here?"

Calista's accusing tone was the first thing he was greeted with as he entered Harlow's apartment, and it made him growl. He was already out of his mind with worry knowing Harlow was out there somewhere, and everyone else seemed to be panicking right along with him. Toby didn't need this shit, too.

Mel walked in behind him seconds later and clapped him on the shoulder. "The more people looking, the better. Right, Calista?" She eyed his woman's best friend and continued to speak. "And he's here because he loves her. He was just too idiotic to figure it out sooner. Don't you, Tob?"

He nodded. "I always knew. I just didn't think I deserved her. Felt guilty, too." He fisted his hands at his sides and faced the woman currently glaring at him. "I want to fix this rift I put between us. I've been working on it for days now, and I'm almost there. I will make this up to Harlow. I swear to every person here, I won't stop till I make it right, and I vow that if I'm lucky enough to get her back, I will move heaven and earth to make her happy. Please tell me you figured out where she might be?"

"Cut him some slack, will you?" Rebel cleared his throat as they walked in. "He's telling you the truth. He asked for our help to pull it off." He pointed toward Carson and back to himself.

Calista eyed Toby the entire time Rebel spoke, as if she was trying to judge his sincerity. Carson moved to put his arm around her, and she seemed to finally relax. "Now can you put the man out of his misery and answer the question?" he asked.

Calista nodded as she looked at the faces around her. Diamond, Melody, Rebel, Carson, and Toby all impatiently waited for her to spill. "I called Twin City earlier, and she didn't drop anything off at the magazine. Said they hadn't seen her at all in a few days, but that's normal. Harlow works her own hours. As long as she makes their deadlines, they don't care much. There are only a few other places I can think of. The coffee shop down the street, Dark Java's. She loves the place. She could be at Lakewood Cemetery, where her daughter is buried, or she could also be wandering Lyndale Park. They're open till midnight, I think. She goes there to unwind and admire the butterflies, hummingbirds, and gardens. Says it's peaceful."

"Okay, I think we should split up. It'll go much quicker," Dee said. "Carson and Rebel can check out Dark Java's. Carson's been there before. Callie and Toby, you should team up and check out Lakewood. See if she went to visit her daughter. Mel, you and me will go to Lyndale together and then meet back up here. First couple of people to find Harlow texts everyone else to let 'em know."

"That's a good idea and all, but someone should probably stay here in case she comes back," Carson replied. "Dee, why don't you stay behind? Mel can come with me to the coffee shop, Reb can go check out the park, and Calista and Toby will still go to the grave. Check it out."

"Let's roll." Toby strode to the door and held it wide for everyone to get going. They had a plan now, and the sooner they went out looking, the better he'd feel. He wanted to quit wasting time.

In their haste to get out of the building, they almost knocked over the person they were set to look for. Carson barreled into Harlow, and she almost fell onto her butt. Thankfully, Rebel caught her before any damage was done. Toby stood there frozen to the spot to check her out, make sure she was okay indeed.

"What are you all doing here?" Harlow looked confused, worn out, and vulnerable. He fucking hated that. Before anyone could respond, his body moved into action without much thought. She was just feet away, and he couldn't help himself. He had to feel her.

"Scared the shit out of me." He pressed his body against hers, cradled the sides of her face as gently as he could, and took her mouth, hungrily and possessively. These last days without her had been torture. After he'd drunk himself stupid the day he confronted her and then his staff, he'd read Harlow's letter to Mel and realized his mistake. This woman in his arms was amazing, his second chance, and for some reason, she wanted him too. Kissing her was as easy as breathing. They just clicked, and it became instinctual. Harlow didn't see it coming, but she reciprocated and gave as good as he did. So there was that.

"Okay, Casanova, enough with the lip lock. I want some answers." Calista crossed her arms and tapped her foot impatiently when Toby pulled back.

Harlow looked dazed now, and his heart swelled.

"Huh?" Harlow shook her head as if to clear cobwebs. "I have no idea what you're talking about. I also don't know why you're all here or why Toby is kissing me again suddenly?" She turned to him, and he winced when she glared.

"You haven't talked to any of us in days, so Calista came over because enough is enough already. We planned a girl's night, but when you didn't show and wouldn't answer your phone, we called the guys to help us look for you. Don't ever do that to us again." Mel wagged a finger at her and abruptly turned to go back inside the building.

"Where were you, anyway?" Toby was curious.

"I-I needed some air, and I hadn't left the apartment in days, so I went to see Lily. I've been meaning to, anyway." She sighed. "Also, my phone died the other day when I was avoiding everyone, and I never bothered to recharge it. It's in my room."

They all climbed the stairs to a waiting Dee, leaning against the apartment's doorframe. "I could hear your voices carry and thought I'd check it out. There's our girl." She winked as Harlow walked past.

"I appreciate your concern, but if you don't mind, I'm kind of tired. Rain check on the girl jam for tonight, okay?" Harlow looked him right in the eye then, and he could see she was still hurting.

Fuck!

"You're all free to go now. Toby…" She gulped and lowered her head, no longer making eye contact. "As you can see, I'll be fine. I'm sorry that you were inconvenienced tonight. I'll make sure no one bothers you again where I'm concerned."

"Well, that's too bad because I'm not having it." Harlow let out a surprised gasp when he threw her over his shoulder and marched them both toward her bedroom for some privacy. "I have some things I need you to hear before you go kicking me out."

Harlow must have been too shocked to protest because she hadn't put up any resistance to follow along. Toby turned to the rest of their entourage and addressed them. "We'll need a few minutes of privacy, so make yourselves comfortable. Shouldn't be too long."

Chapter Twenty-Nine

HARLOW

She watched as her friends all gave them a thumbs up and headed to her living room. Toby entered her room, kicked the door shut, and gently sat her on the bed. He stood in front of her. "Listen, Toby. I'm so emotionally drained right now, I don't have it in me to fight with you. At least not tonight. What do you want?"

She crossed her arms and turned her head to look away, focusing instead on one of Lily's photos on her nightstand. Her heart felt as if it had an open wound, and looking at Toby made it ache.

"Christ," Toby cursed. "I'm such an idiot."

Harlow gave him a curt nod. Although she could understand that he was probably trying to protect himself the other day, it was a misguided attempt. He was a fool for the way he treated her. Fool or not, she loved him. Didn't mean she was going to make this easy on him.

"I deserve that." He sighed, and the bed dipped

when he sat beside her. She tensed when he reached for her hand, and she felt so vulnerable. He'd nearly crushed her spirit when he walked out, and now this. She was so confused, hurt, and angry. Was he toying with her? Since visiting with her daughter, her emotions were all over the place.

"Could you look at me, please?" he asked. He cupped the side of her face and gently moved her head so she'd look at him. "That a girl. Much better now."

Harlow closed her eyes. She needed a minute to gather her thoughts, then she opened them again. "When did you get the new tattoo?" Toby lowered his hand and looked at his wrist. She'd noticed the sunflower now inked there and was curious.

"Look familiar?" Toby gave her a sad smile and touched the flower now etched onto his skin.

"Should it?" she asked, examining it more closely.

"Yeah, because it's yours." Toby cleared his throat. "I kept your drawing the night I taught you to draw the flower. You seemed so proud of it that it became special to me. Got it framed and put it on my mantle." He shrugged. "Would you believe me if I told you I knew I made a mistake almost the minute I walked out your door? I'm a jackass, Harlow, but I was just so angry after I found that letter. Trust doesn't come easily for me, and I'm messed up. I fucked up, period, especially with you. Mel fessed to writing it and going to you. I know now that it was kept personal. Should have took your word for it the first time, but I was scared. You terrified me because you made me feel things I had only felt for one other woman. It made me wonder if I was betraying her for being with you. I became happy again, and I didn't feel like I deserved it. After I read your response to Mel, I got drunk, cried, and passed out. The next day, I gave myself your sunflower as a reminder of you always. Like it or not, you're a part of me, Harlow, and I don't want to let you go."

Toby choked up on the last words, and she gulped as she tried to stop her own tears from flowing. She'd cried enough in the last week to last her a lifetime. "What's the plan now? You hurt me, Toby. I told you I love you and you crushed me. Incinerated my heart and walked out. How do I know that won't happen again? Especially when you can't even say it back. I can't compete with a ghost."

"You don't have to." Toby got onto his knees and crawled in front of her. He grasped her two hands in his as if he was afraid she'd run away and pleaded, "I do love you, Harlow, but I don't expect you to believe me right now. I plan to prove it to you, and I'm not giving up, so I'm begging you not to give up on me just yet. I get that I have issues, and I've set up an appointment to deal with them. I meet with Dr. Hartley the day after tomorrow for the first time. My physician recommended him. Told me he was a good shrink to talk to. I would love for you to come with me to a session, at some point, if you want to."

"Oh, Toby." Harlow blew out a big breath she'd been holding and smiled through watery eyes. "I'm happy for you. Dr. Hartley has established a great reputation. I'm proud of you for taking that step. It hurts me to say this because of my deep feelings for you, but I need some time to figure things out. I need to know that you're with me for me, one hundred percent." She cried, and her shoulders shook as she ripped her hands away from his and brought them up to hide her face. Her heart beat faster when she felt his arms embrace her, and she savored that moment while she could. "I just need time."

"I can give you that," he said. Harlow looked up when she heard Toby's sniffle. He wiped his eyes on his sleeve to dry them. "But I've given you enough words tonight. Now it's time for actions. As God is my witness, by the time I'm done wooing you back to me, you will have no doubt that you're it. My second chance, and my forever."

Toby leaned over to kiss her on the forehead, lingering there before he placed one last peck on top of her head. He opened the door and looked back. "Take all of the time you need, but I'll be in touch, Harlow. I love you." The last part was on a whisper as he shut the door, and she found herself all alone again, listening to murmurs in the other room.

She flopped back on the bed and curled into a ball. Her apartment became silent, and she figured everyone was gone.

Calista knocked softly before announcing herself. She climbed onto the bed and spooned herself around Harlow from behind. Harlow appreciated the support. It'd been a long day, but tomorrow was a new one and a new start. Her fingers were crossed that Toby meant what he'd said, but only time would tell.

Chapter Thirty

Dear Harlow:

My boyfriend's ex just moved back to Minneapolis after working abroad for a couple years. In fact, the reason they broke up was because they couldn't make the long-distance thing work for very long.

Every time we go out, she seems to be there, as they have many mutual friends. She gets too friendly, and I hate it. We've been together about eight months, and I know I should feel secure in our relationship. I love him, but how do I compete with his ex when I know he still has feelings for her? You can see it whenever she's around. I've tried talking to him about it, but I get nowhere. Help me Harlow. I'm going crazy here.

Sincerely,

~Troubled Girlfriend~

*

Dear Troubled Girlfriend:
The answer to your question is you don't.
There should be no contest. Although I can
empathize with feeling like you need to
compete. The ex is his past, and you're his
present. Sounds to me like you need to let your
boyfriend know your concerns again until he
listens. Both about his feelings for the ex-
girlfriend and about the disrespect you're given
when she gets too friendly. If he has any
respect for you and your relationship, he
should put a stop to it. I'm sure if the tables
were turned, he wouldn't be happy with this
situation, either. I wish you the best of luck,
and if all else fails, you may need to dump him.
My heart goes out to you,
Harlow

***

HARLOW

There was nothing like the classics. Richard
Gere was currently on TV, picking up a very sexy-
looking Julia Roberts in a fancy sports car. Say
hello to the hooker meeting the gorgeous rich guy in
this old school forbidden love story called *Pretty
Woman*. Harlow sighed; if only it was as simple as
in the movies. At least then, you were guaranteed a

213

happily ever after, and she wanted one of those for herself.

She picked up a handful of chocolate M&M's and passed the popcorn bowl to Mel. A few days had passed since Toby had vowed to woo her, and she hadn't heard from him since. It was depressing, yet she did ask for time. Words were one thing, actions were quite another, and she had to guard her heart better. Had to know for certain that Toby was ready to move on. Thankfully, she was currently in good company to distract herself from this funk she'd been struggling with.

Girl's night, yeah!

"Damn, that Richard Gere is hot, for an older dude." Dee wiggled her eyebrows suggestively as she poured them each a glass of margaritas from a big pitcher. After she finished passing them out, she set the jug on the coffee table and sat down with flourish. "This night has been long overdue. It's nice to unwind with my peeps."

"Agreed," Harlow said. She dropped a bunch of the little round, candied chocolates in her mouth and chewed. "Thanks for being here, you guys. I really don't know what I'd do without you. I know I've been a recluse in the last week, and I appreciate your patience with me."

"Well, we love you." Calista held her glass up. "Let's toast to the good things in our lives. Here's to great friends, booze, a bunch of junk food, and the fantasy men we admire in these chick flicks. May we one day find our own true loves, and may they cherish us like the goddesses we know we are."

"Couldn't have said it better myself. Although I

might add a salute to the good men out there who learn from their mistakes. Everyone deserves a second chance." Mel clinked her glass against Harlow's as Dee and Calista did the same.

Dee snorted before she took a sip. "Very subtle, Mel."

"I'm sorry, okay." Melody looked at Harlow with wide eyes. "I know he's a dipshit once in a while, but I'm rooting for the two of you. You're good for each other, and if it's any consolation, he's been just as miserable without you."

Harlow took another sip from her glass and sighed. "I'm rooting for us as well. I love him, but this experience made me realize I need to tread carefully. I need to know one hundred percent that he's moved on before we can be together again. I'm sure Carley was a very lovely person. I've only heard great things about her, but I can't continue to compete with her memory. I deserve better than that."

"Nobody can fault you for feeling that way," Dee said. "Carley was good people, and it's tragic what happened to her. I also know she'd want Toby to be happy, and you're it. It's like comparing apples and oranges. They're both different but equally tasty."

"It's good to know I'm tasty." Harlow shrugged, and they all had a giggle. She put down her drink when her phone started to vibrate. It was in her pocket, and she took it out. "Speak of the Devil. Toby just texted me." Her heart beat quicker, and she got that excited feeling in the pit of her belly when she opened it. It was butterflies.

"What does it say?" Calista asked. Each woman

seemed to sit up straighter as if eagerly waiting for her to reply.

She clicked on the text and read it out loud. "It says: *I meant every word I said the other night. My step one to win you back was the sunflower tattoo. It was made special knowing that you were the one to draw it for me. Proof that you can draw with the right teacher beside you, and now that memory will live on always. My step two was the kiss I gave you the moment we locked eyes again after I'd been such an idiot. I was just so relieved you were okay. I poured all my feelings into that lip lock and kissing you was as easy as breathing. I long to do that again sometime soon. Now, this is my step three. Please click on the link. I'll do whatever it takes, as long as it takes me, to make you believe. All my love, Toby.*"

"Wow!" Calista clutched her chest, while Mel and Dee gave each other a high five. "What's the link for?"

"Yeah, click on it already. We want to see it too." Melody looked excited for her, and Harlow chuckled.

"Whatever it is, it's on YouTube." The girls leaned over her shoulder to peek, while Harlow rubbed her hands together and clicked away with bated breath. Ash Harris's face filled the screen, and she squealed. She was a huge fan of Love the Sinner, and to have the lead singer addressing you on the internet was a dream come true. What was Toby up to, and why was it his cousin's face she was looking at and not his?

Calista shushed her.

216

Mel rolled her eyes. "Ash gets this reaction all of the time. It's all good, girlfriend."

But Harlow ignored them, entranced inside her own little world that included this intriguing video Toby wanted to share with her. She turned up the volume.

"Hello, Harlow Ross. I hear you're a huge fan, and I can't tell you how humbled I am to know it. I could tell from the moment Toby mentioned you, you were somebody worth knowing. It takes a special woman to knock my cousin to his knees, and I know that must not have been an easy task. You both seem to have a lot in common, from what I hear, and a unique understanding of each other. He tells me you make him want to be a better man. And, let me tell you, Toby is one of the good ones. It's why I was excited to help him pull this off. I hope you're listening closely before I pass you back to him because Toby loves you from the bottom of his heart. Take it from me." Ash finished with a wink. "I'm currently still on tour, but as soon as we can manage it, the band and I would love to meet you. Until then, I present to you, Toby James, everyone."

The camera moved away from Ash and onto Toby's lone figure. He was sitting on a stool with a guitar in hand, and Harlow felt like she melted on the spot at the sight of him.

"Hey, Harlow. I know you're a huge fan of the band, and I thought it might mean something special to hear Ash speak as if he knows you already. I also figured it might help this post reach more people if Love the Sinner's prodigy was on it.

His fan base has a far better outreach than mine does. Local tattooist with an old show." Toby pointed at himself. "And the rock star. I love you, baby, so much, and I'd like the whole world to know it. Hence the video, my step number three, but there's more…" Toby's face lit up with hope as he gave her his signature smirk, and her heart soared with happiness. "Ash and I also co-wrote this song for you that I'm about to sing for the very first time. You ready to hear it?" The moment Toby started playing the guitar, she wasn't the only one in tears. The whole apartment was. Calista, Mel, and Dee joined her. While she suspected theirs were tears of envy, hers were of complete joy. She hadn't remembered ever being so jubilant before. It was incredible, and she absorbed every word he sang. If this wasn't proof enough that he loved her, then nothing would be.

Drifted alone as an empty shell
My scars burned while I was in hell
Took women to bed
I was distracted with dread
A shallow escape to quell the pain
Loves were lost and a new one was gained
I was absent and alone but no more
You showed me I deserve to feel more

I'm ready to say goodbye to the past
You're going to be my second chance
My lady to love forever and more
So here I am reaching out to you
You're holding my heart

FOREVER WITH YOU

It's yours to store
You showed me I deserve to feel more

Continuing to run would be insane
I want to be with you to dance in the rain
To hold your hand, to cherish, and kiss you
When you're not around I ache, and I miss you
It breaks me to see you cry
I'd rather see us both fly
When I look in your eyes
And my arms go around you
I know I'm in bliss
And thank God that I've found you

So, baby hear my plea
You're it for me
You give me the will and strength to continue
I've found my forever
to infinity and a day
My love will never go away

Like a sunflower on a beautiful day
Together we shine bright
please don't push me away
With visions of our future where we're holding
hands
I'll show you I'm strong enough to be your man

I'm ready to say goodbye to the past
You're going to be my second chance
My lady to love forever and more
I'll do what it takes to show you I'm yours

Baby hear me plea
You're it for me
When you're by my side
There isn't a need to hide
I'm ready to be the man you need

Girl, you showed me I deserve to feel more
The past is lost, and the future is what I'm looking
for
You showed me I deserve to feel more
That I deserve to feel more
I love you

"Oh my God!" Calista fanned her face. "That was amazing."

"Harlow," Mel gasped. "I've never seen Toby like that before. It's like the words bled right out of him. They were so heartfelt and personal."

"That right there is your proof." Dee enthusiastically pointed at Harlow's phone. "He's finally ready to move on."

"I have to see him." Harlow jumped up from the couch and cradled the phone to her chest. "I've got to go." She raced around the apartment to grab her jacket, keys, and shoes. She threw open the door and paused. "Stay as long as you like. Callie has her key to lock up, and I'll keep you posted. If all goes well, I won't be texting until sometime tomorrow." She winked as her entourage whistled and clapped with excitement.

"Go get him, girl."

Harlow rushed down the stairs, taking them two at a time, and nearly tripped over her own two feet in her haste to get to the car. She started the ignition and prayed that he was home.

Chapter Thirty-One

TOBY

Toby began pacing his apartment the minute he'd sent the text, and a million and one questions bombarded his thoughts.

Was she watching it?

Did she like it?

Did she finally believe him?

Would she take him back?

And if she didn't, what could he possibly do to top that?

He'd shout out his love from the rooftops if that's what Harlow needed from him. Contacting Ash to ask for some help seemed to be a good idea at the time. This video would hopefully tell the world. It hadn't been online for very long, and the viewings already surpassed six figures. It was crazy. He shook his head and picked up his sketch pad. Ten minutes later, and he was still looking at the blank page. He gave up, tossed the pad on the coffee table, and sat forward with a sigh. The suspense was killing him.

Come on, baby. Call me. Tell me you watched it and loved it.

His phone made a noise, signalling a notification, and he lunged for it on the cushion beside him.

Mel: If you're not home, you might want to get there pronto. Your girl saw the video, and she's on her way. Good job, Tob. Harlow couldn't get out of here fast enough. I'm so glad you've finally found your happy. Proud of you too.

After reading it, Toby smirked and gave himself a mental high five. He looked around the apartment and quickly straightened up. He gathered his dinner dishes and dropped them in the sink. He quickly wiped the counters and threw the rag back on the counter when he finished. It'd have to do. Toby looked around, satisfied now that the place looked decent enough. But what about him? He turned to sniff his pits and sighed with relief. He smelled decent but now felt anxious. This was it.

Within a couple of minutes, there was an insistent pounding on the door, and he knew it was her. His heart raced, and he eagerly opened it. No words were exchanged. The moment they locked eyes, she pounced, and it caught him off guard. She jumped up, threw her arms around his shoulders, and wrapped her legs around his hips. Toby fell backward, taking the brunt of the fall, while she peppered kisses all over his face. It shocked him.

"I'm so sorry. Please tell me you're not hurt."

Harlow scrambled to get up and held out her hand to help him do the same. The moment he stood, his arms went around her again. She was magnetic, and he couldn't stop touching her if he tried. Didn't want to.

Harlow's gaze ran from his feet to the top of his head, checking him out. Her hands rested against his heart, and he couldn't help but smile. She was right where he wanted her to be. "I'm fine, Harlow, promise. In fact, I'm now more than fine." He bent down to rest his forehead against hers and whispered, "It's so good to see you again."

Her whole face lit up at his words, and he cherished the moment. "It's good to see you too. Toby, I feel like it's my turn to apologize. When you walked out on me, I was shattered."

"Har—"

Harlow held up her hand and took a step back, leaving Toby no choice but to drop both of his arms to his sides. He fisted his hands to keep from reaching out. "Please let me finish," she said. "You have to understand, when I first met you, I could feel this pull. I was attracted to you, of course, but there was more to it. You're so talented and hard-working; you're successful and likeable, the whole package, but you were also damaged and hurting. It's a trait I can understand well because I am too, in my own way. You got me, though, and still do. It's like we're two imperfect puzzle pieces but put us together and we fit. I just couldn't help but love you, but in the back of my mind, there was always this insecurity. You never promised me anything permanent, but I wanted it badly." She shrugged.

"When you found the letter and walked out, I thought I'd never be able to compete with Carley. She was the love of your life, a-and I'm just me. I guess what I'm trying to say is, I decided to protect my heart. The other night when you tried to tell me how you felt…God, Toby, I'm so sorry." She rushed forward and began to kiss him all over his face again. It was adorable. "I." Kiss. "Love." Kiss. "You, so much." Kiss. "And I know you love me. That video was the sweetest, sincerest, most incredible thing anyone has ever done for me." Kiss. Kiss.

Toby gulped and gave her a nod. He needed a minute to compose himself. He hugged her tightly and smiled. "Finally. I honestly didn't know how I was going to top the song. When we met, I think my problem was that I could see our dark, and I let mine consume me. Been living with mine for too long. The difference was yours had holes all over it, letting the light shine through, and I was drawn to you. I know you're still grieving your daughter, but you don't let it eat at you like I did when I lost Carley. Despite it, you help people every day. I'd wish for anything to get you your daughter back and keep that hurt away, and I'm so sorry I don't have that ability. One thing I can give you is me, though. I swear to you from this day forward, if you give me that chance, I'll make it my mission to love, protect, and cherish you for as long as you'll let me."

"Toby…" Harlow looked up with tears in her eyes.

"It's my turn to finish." He pressed a finger to her lips. "When I lost Carley, it took a part of me.

Not going to lie to you. I wanted an eternity, and it was ripped away the first time. So when you came along, and I saw Mel's letter, I used that shit as an excuse to push you away. Why? Because from the moment I saw you in my lobby at Misfit, I could see you were special. You made me feel things I didn't want to. Suddenly, my dark began to crack, and I had light in my life again. I wasn't drowning in grief because I had you with me. It freaked me out some. I fucked up, Harlow, and I'm not perfect, so I'm going to probably screw up again at some point. However, I do know without a doubt that if you give me that second chance, I'll make sure you know there isn't anything or anybody to compete with from this day forward. I love you that much."

"I believe you." Harlow nodded her head and grinned. "Now that we've both said our piece, can we please get to the love making?"

"Missed you," he said. Toby kissed her to show her how much. Speaking his feelings wasn't something he excelled at, except with Harlow. Showing her them like she requested, however, was in a more comfortable territory. He'd gladly oblige.

Let the sparks ignite.

The moment his mouth crashed down on hers, the kiss went eager and hard. She nipped his bottom lip, and he moaned, loving the slight sting before she soothed it with her tongue. Toby broke the kiss for a few seconds to yank her shirt off and threw it behind him. He did the same with his own. With a flick of his fingers, he had her bra unhooked, and Harlow finished the honors by working her arms free. The lacy undergarment fell to their feet. He

226

pulled her closer and took her mouth again. The feel of her skin against his was phenomenal. Her nipples were hard, and he groaned as Harlow ran her finger nails down his back. He loved that signature move. She gasped as his lips trailed against her jaw. "I want you so badly, Toby."

Those words were like music to his ears. He grunted and kissed his way down her throat, could feel her pulse beat as frantically as his was. "So beautiful," he mumbled. Harlow moved her leg up to his waist and thrust against him where they stood. He gripped her bottom, and her other leg wrapped around him as well. Her hands played in his hair while her arms were wrapped around his neck, and he pressed his forehead against hers again. They were both panting, and it gave them a moment to catch their breath.

Toby walked with her until his legs hit the side of his bed. He gently lowered her down on the mattress before climbing on top. He tucked some hair behind her ears and lovingly caressed her face. "I have the world in the palm of my hands right now. My world is right here." He quickly kissed her lips. "Love you, baby."

"Oh, Toby," Harlow whispered with emotion. "I lo-ove you too." She hissed the last part and writhed against him. His left hand palmed one breast while his mouth worshiped the other. Once he paid equal attention to both, he kissed his way down her stomach and gripped the waistband of her pants to get rid of them, underwear and all. Toby stood to admire the view, wanting to commit this very moment to memory. Harlow was a vision fully clothed, but get her naked, and she blew his mind.

Mine.

"Say it again," Toby said. He could see the love in her eyes when she looked at him, but he needed to hear the words before they went further.

"I love you, Mr. James." Harlow partially sat up and eyed his straining erection with interest, and she licked her lips.

"And who do you belong with?" Harlow looked at him again when he asked the question, and she maintained eye contact as she answered with sincerity.

"I belong with you, Toby. I'm yours and you're mine."

"Damn straight," he said.

He grabbed her thighs to spread her wide and dove in to taste her. He felt like a starving man in need of sustenance, and she was his favorite flavored dessert. He loved this pussy. It was glistening and smooth, sticky sweet. He licked her slow at first to savor the moment. He tongued her opening, tasted around her slick folds, and lapped at her clit repeatedly. Her fingers went through his hair, and she moved her hips eagerly against his face. Her juices dripped from his chin while he licked, flicked, and fucked her with his tongue. Her taste became more potent the wetter she became, and he knew she was close the minute she yanked on his hair to move him precisely where she needed him.

"Please, Toby, I'm almost there."

He smiled against her and obliged her request. His head moved side to side while he played with her clit, and then up and down. He took the bud into his mouth and sucked it.

"Oh God, so fucking good," she cried out. He looked up, and her chest rapidly rose and fell. Her eyes were closed, and he'd become mesmerized as he worked her into bliss. This woman was amazing, and all his. It felt like his heart was expanding. He was so happy. Her eyes popped open, they locked with his, and she gripped his head tighter to her core. Her legs began to shake, and her moans were louder. "I'm coming, Toby. Fuck me, I'm c-oming!"

Harlow erupted like an active volcano, and it turned him on so much, he was ready to cream in his pants like a freaking newbie.

Toby stood while Harlow recovered, and he ripped his pants off, almost tripping in his haste to free his cock. He was aching so bad. A couple of weeks apart felt torturous. He may be pathetic, but he also didn't care. He sighed with relief the minute he was free and grabbed a condom from his drawer.

"Here, allow me." Harlow winked and reached for it. She tore open the wrapper with her teeth and quickly put it on him. "Now we're talking." She stretched out and turned around to get on all fours. She looked back and smiled while he admired the view of her bum in the air. "Love me, Toby. I feel empty without you."

Toby grabbed her hips and pulled her closer to the edge of the bed. He stood behind her and palmed her ass before smacking it. He squeezed her cheek again, grabbed the base of his dick, and rubbed his tip between her folds. At her opening, he paused and slowly sunk in. They moaned in unison the moment he was balls deep and began to move. It felt amazing. Her cunt was wet, snug, and warm. So soft, and incredible. He gripped her hips and flexed his fingers, trying desperately not to blow too soon. He fucked her fast, then slowed down, fast and slow some more. He leaned forward to kiss her back, and it gave her goose bumps. He licked her skin. "You feel incredible Harlow." He stopped, pulled out, and flipped her over. "But tonight, I want to look in your eyes." Her boobs bounced when he entered her, and he could feel her fingernails dig into his shoulders leaving their mark. The familiar sounds of their moans and skin slapping skin filled the air, muting the TV at the other end of the loft. He was so close now and made sure to rub against her clit every time he pumped out and back in. He wanted to reach ecstasy together this time.

"Toby." Harlow's back arched, and he gasped the moment she let go. Her walls tightened and spasmed around his shaft. Ripple after ripple of pleasure consumed him, and his cock jerked with the force of his own orgasm. It left him boneless.

"Uh, Toby?" Harlow pushed at his shoulders and giggled. "I love having you on top of me. But you're getting heavy."

"Sorry," he mumbled. Toby rolled over onto his side, taking her with him. They were face to face, laying in the middle of his bed and satisfied. She kissed his chest and rubbed the spot with her fingers.

"Are you okay?"

"I've never been better," he said. Toby took the

hand she used to rub his chest and brought her fingers to his lips, pecking each one.

"Me too." Harlow smiled. "What comes next?"

Toby shrugged. "We're official. I say we enjoy tonight and tell the others tomorrow." He nudged her chin with his forefinger and stared. "We still take it one day at a time, baby, but with more confidence in our future. I'm in this for the long haul. I want forever with you."

"I'd like that. You have no idea how much." Harlow squealed and hugged him tightly. Toby chuckled and pried her arms from around him. He held them above her head and leaned over to kiss her lips. Only this time, there was no hurry. She wasn't going anywhere, and neither was he. He was finally beginning to heal, to seek help, and most importantly he found love again. As the misery of his past lessened, it was replaced by a new hope, and he looked forward to their journey ahead, together.

Epilogue

CARSON

"Here's the happy couple now." He clapped his hands and got up to give Toby a pat on the back. "It's good to see you, man."

Before Toby could respond, Carson took Harlow from his friend's arms and gave her a big hug. "Damn, Harlow. Are we at Fanny's or in a museum? Because the moment you walked in, it was like looking at a true work of art."

"Oh, Carson, I hope you never change." Harlow chuckled and pinched his cheek.

"What can I say?" Carson winked. "I'm the best."

"Hey." Toby grabbed Harlow by her belt loops and pulled her by his side. "Get your own woman. This one is spoken for."

Carson laughed.

"Yeah, yeah." Mel pushed her brother aside. "You could at least let them take a seat so the rest of us can congratulate them."

Carson shrugged. *Whatever.*

It'd been a few days since their favorite couple reunited, and tonight they were out to celebrate. Toby sat between him and Rebel, and Mel dragged Harlow to the other side to sit across from them between the girls. No doubt to get the dirt or whatever girly shit women talked about. He took a sip of his beer and observed the crowd.

"I know I've probably said this before, but happy looks good on you," Dee exclaimed. "It took you long enough to text."

"We were busy." Toby smiled when Harlow blushed. "Had to make up for lost time."

Rebel snorted. "Lucky bastard."

"Don't I know it." Toby chuckled, and Carson could feel the envy in the pit of his stomach. At thirty-one, he was young enough still and having fun, but the one-night stands were beginning to get old, and he couldn't wait to find his own Harlow. Well, not her, obviously, but a woman who could bring him to his knees. A woman he could see himself spending more time with than a night or two, but he was beginning to think she didn't exist.

Maybe that's why he'd been spending a lot of nights at The Busy Beaver lately instead of hooking up. The moment that stripper Lacey stepped on the stage, a spark had ignited with just one look. There was a pull there every single time she performed, but for some reason, he couldn't get her to give him a lap dance. She didn't do them, apparently, and it frustrated the fuck out of him. Maybe it was the thrill of the chase that intrigued him. Who knew? But who found forever with a stripper anyway?

Mel kicked him under the table, and he glared. *Fuck, that hurt.*

She mouthed, "Are you okay?"

Carson nodded. He looked around the table, and it looked like Rebel was putting the moves on Dee again, and Toby was leaning across the table talking with Harlow in hushed tones, paying no attention to the brother and sister duo.

"I'm fine, what's up?" Carson leaned back in his chair and folded his arms, like he didn't have a care in the world.

"Nothing, you just looked way too serious over there. Lost in thoughts." Mel leaned forward and clasped her hands together. "You know you can talk to me about anything, right?"

He nodded. "I do, but I'm good, so stop with the serious talk already. We're here to celebrate. Who needs another drink?" He waved his empty in the air and stood, not bothering to listen to anyone's reply. "I'll get another round."

Carson walked away, and he sighed as Mel caught up with him.

"Thought I'd help you carry them back," she said, but he knew better. There really was something to this twin intuition thing, and she wasn't backing down.

"I told you I'm fine, Mel, and I am. I'm just adjusting. I'm glad for Toby. Harlow's good for him, and he deserves his happy ending. I guess I just wish I could find mine." He grimaced and pointed a finger at her. "Don't you dare tell anybody I said that. You do, and I'll tell them about that time you flashed Dee's uncle when he visited

234

last spring."

Mel narrowed her eyes. "Don't you dare." And he laughed as she did some pointing of her own right in the middle of his chest. "I was drunk. It didn't go any further than that, and Dee would kill me if she found out."

"My lips are sealed as long as yours are." Carson shrugged then turned to flag down Fanny's old man. "Hey, Harold. Six of the usual."

When he turned around, Mel was smiling with a wicked gleam in her eyes. She was up to something, but what? He looked at her curiously but didn't have to wait for much longer to hear her spill the beans.

"You'll never guess who I talked to today."

Like he cared. "Who did you talk to today?" He casually leaned against the bar and played along.

"Tate. She's back, Carson, and she's here to stay."

Tate?

That one word alone had his palms sweating. "You don't say."

Mel nodded enthusiastically and rubbed her hands together.

Tate Owens was Mel's best friend since childhood. She moved away shortly after high school to go to some fancy place in New York, a dance school, and he hadn't seen her since. She was Mel's exact opposite. Mel was loud, Tate was quiet. Mel liked attention, Tate preferred to stay invisible. She was shy, sweet, and tried hard to hide her beauty back then, but Carson saw. Oh yeah, he saw what she tried to hide, and Mel knew it too. Only he

235

hadn't acted on his desires when they were younger. Tate was different from the girls he was used to. She deserved the world, and he wasn't done playing the field, therefore he didn't go there. As tempting as it could have been. "Good for her." He cleared his throat. "I mean, it'll be great to see her again."

"I'll bet." Mel doubled over as she laughed and wiped her eyes when she was upright again. "You keep on pretending that doesn't mean something to you. You know, she had the biggest crush on you, as well, right?"

Carson rolled his eyes again, not willing to take the bait. "That was high school, Mel. Grow the fuck up."

Mel ignored him. "She plans to open her own choreography studio and teach dance. Has some other job in the meantime…"

Carson turned to grab the beers Harold had put in front of him and ignored his sister right back while they returned to their table.

"Took you long enough." Toby stood to help pass them out, and Carson held out his bottle to make a toast. "To Toby and Harlow."

The table chorused him, and he chugged half the bottle in one go.

Tate Owens. Damn.

He had a feeling life was about to become more interesting. He could feel Mel's stare, and when he looked over, she smirked.

Fucking sister. A pain in my ass.

He flipped her the finger and slammed the bottle down on the table. She was up to something, and he had a feeling it had to do with the woman he now couldn't stop thinking about.

Fanny walked up to the table with a bunch of food, and his stomach growled. There were wings, nachos, fries, and a plate of burgers by the time she was done. "I just love feeding you kids." Fanny smiled. "Tonight, it's on the house."

Carson clutched his chest to lay it on thick before Fanny walked away. Flirting just came naturally to him, and he couldn't help himself. "Mamma Deuce, would you touch my arm before you go?"

The old lady knew him well and chuckled. She rested her hand on his bicep. "Now what?"

He winked. "Now I get to tell all of my friends I was touched by an angel."

"Oh, shut up." She swatted him playfully and laughed as she left them.

Nothing would be on the house tonight because he'd make sure to tip her enough to cover it all, but first, it was time to fill his belly and continue to mingle.

Tonight was about his friends. Tomorrow, he'd worry about everything else.

***

If you enjoyed *Forever with You* stay tuned for Carson Tyler and Tate Owens's story in *Hearts and Headboards (Misfit Tattoo Book 2)*. It's in the works.

In the meantime, don't forget to check out The Bad Girls Series, *Chasing Butterflies* and *Cowgirl Crazy*. Both Books are only $.99 and flow with this

story.
Happy Reading!

"Here's to the crazy ones. The misfits. The rebels. The troublemakers. The round pegs in the square holes. The ones who see things differently. They're not fond of rules. And they have no respect for the status quo. You can quote them, disagree with them, glorify or vilify them. About the only thing you can't do is ignore them. Because they change things. They push the human race forward. And while some may see them as the crazy ones, we see genius. Because the people who are crazy enough to think they can change the world, are the ones who do."

~Rob Siltanen

About the Author

Jennifer Labelle resides in Canada with her husband and three beautiful children. After her third child she became a stay at home mom. In her busy household Jennifer likes to spend her down time engrossed in the stories that she creates. She is an active reader of romance, mystery and anything paranormal. With an education in Addictions work she's decided to take a less stressful approach in life and hopes that you enjoy, as she shares some of her imagination and artistic inspiration with all of you.

Facebook:
https://www.facebook.com/pages/Author-Jennifer-Labelle/168414043184292

Twitter:
https://twitter.com/1JenniferLabell

Goodreads:
https://www.goodreads.com/author/show/4649930.Jennifer_Labelle

Website:
http://www.jenniferlabelle.com/

Google Plus:
https://plus.google.com/u/0/110192794885898998367/posts

Bookbub:
https://www.bookbub.com/profile/jennifer-labelle

Also, please consider leaving a review. It's greatly appreciated and helps authors spread the word about their work.

Thank you!

Join our Reader Group on Facebook and don't miss out on meeting our authors and entering epic giveaways!

Limitless Reading

Where reading a book
is your first step to becoming

limitless...

LIMITLESS PUBLISHING *Reader Group*

Join today! *"Where reading a book is your first step to becoming limitless..."*

https://www.facebook.com/groups/LimitlessReading/